THE LIFE OF RE[...]

ANGHARAD PRICE is a novelist, critic and translator, and now Senior Lecturer in the School of Welsh at Bangor University. Her first novel, *Tania'r Tacsi*, was published in 1999, followed in 2002 by *O! Tyn y Gorchudd*, translated here as *The Life of Rebecca Jones*. This second novel was awarded the Prose Medal at the 2002 National Eisteddfod and named Book of the Year by the Welsh Arts Council in 2003. A third novel, *Caersaint*, was shortlisted for the Welsh Arts Council Book of the Year in 2011.

LLOYD JONES is a translator and writer whose novel *Mr Cassini* was the winner of the Welsh Arts Council Book of the Year in 2007.

"The most fascinating and wonderful book"   JAN MORRIS

"It is not easy to put into the customary admiring words what I felt as I read Angharad Price's astonishing novel. Perhaps an admiration verging on awe. A great addition to rural literature" RONALD BLYTHE

"Price's unaffected prose, interspersed with hymnic descriptions of Maesglasau, beautifully evokes a lifestyle that, like the Welsh language, is under threat. Price's bardic voice should go some way to ensuring their preservation".

FRANCESCA ANGELINI, *The Sunday Times*

"A work of grace, beauty and great feeling . . . that moves the heart and fills the head with deeply felt reflections on kin and culture"

PÓL Ó MUIRÍ, *Irish Times*

"This calm, powerful tale of a rural family coping with tragedy and constant flux, has brought Welsh-language fiction to new audiences"

TOM PAYNE, *Daily Telegraph*

"Biography and fiction are beautifully balanced in Angharad Price's gently re-imagined family memoir"

EILEEN BATTERSBY, *Irish Times* Weekend Magazine

"The ending will make you want to turn right back to the beginning"

KATE SAUNDERS, *The Times*

"When you have finished the book . . . you will be in a state of exaltation that is conferred by the numinous"

ELSPETH BARKER, *Literary Review*

"Price's book achieves a rare feat indeed. A lovingly crafted account of Welsh-speaking rural life on the brink of dissolution or at least transformation, it serves both as a touching, tender document and as a thoroughly artful exercise in storytelling – one that, in methods and motifs, can claim a place on the shelf beside Berger, Sebald and Ondaatje. Widely hailed as the first Welsh classic of the 21st century, it now stands tall – whether great-aunt Rebecca would have liked it or not – as a peak of modern British writing too"

BOYD TONKIN, *Independent*

ANGHARAD PRICE

THE LIFE OF REBECCA JONES

A NOVEL

Translated from the Welsh by
Lloyd Jones

with an Afterword by
Jane Aaron

MACLEHOSE PRESS
QUERCUS · LONDON

First published in the Welsh language as *O! Tyn y Gorchudd*
by Gomer Press, Ceredigion, in 2002

Published in 2012 by MacLehose Press

This paperback edition published in 2014 by

MacLehose Press
an imprint of Quercus
55 Baker Street
7th Floor, South Block
London W1U 8EW

A CIP catalogue record for this book is available
from the British Library.

PB ISBN 978 0 85738 712 7

10 9 8 7 6 5

Designed and typeset in Minion by Libanus Press
Printed and bound in Great Britain by Clays Ltd, St Ives plc

This volume is dedicated to Lewis Jones,
and in memory of Olwen Jones (1917–99)

Heartfelt thanks to all family members of Tynybraich,
and to Dafydd Wyn Jones, Blaen Plwyf, Mallwyd,
for their willing co-operation

*A guide to the pronunciation of consonants and vowel
combinations in Welsh can be found on p.160*

Where there is scarcity and deficiency in these meditations, let the considerate reader enlarge upon them according to his own mind.

Hugh Jones (Maesglasau),
Cydymaith yr Hwsmon (*The Companion to Husbandry*), 1774

To this he replied, that there was a book wherein he was in the habit of reading constantly, which contained in it three pages: Heaven, Earth and water; and the creatures therein were merely letters, signifying things unseen.

Hugh Jones, *Cydymaith yr Hwsmon*, 1774

Who created tranquillity? Who formed that which is unheard, unseen and untouched, that which cannot be tasted nor smelled?

This was a reversal of creation. The perfection of an absence.

Tranquillity can belong to one place, yet it ranges the world. It is tied to every passing hour, yet everlasting. It encompasses the exceptional and the commonplace. It connects interior with exterior.

The creator of tranquillity was the guardian of paradox.

From the moment of conception until the moment of death, tranquillity is within and without us. But in the tumult of life it is not easily felt. It shies away from our inflamed senses and all physical excitement; it recoils from our birth cries, from the rush of light to the eye and from the fond indulgence of our loved ones, salty tears and sweet kisses, our earth-bound corruption and putrescence, the ghastly grunt of death . . .

When our senses are spent we seek tranquillity again. And as we age, our search for it becomes more passionate, though never easier.

I too have sought peace throughout my life. I've encountered it, many times – a transparency between myself and the world – only to lose it again. But now I feel myself closing in on a more lasting silence; and I will find it before I die. My eyesight dwindles and my hearing fails. What else should I expect, at my age? But neither blindness nor deafness can perfect the quietness which is about to fall on this valley.

I have raised a temple to tranquillity amid the ruined home-steads of Cwm Maesglasau. I have idolised it in the valley's stream as it whispers past, and as the flow disappears into the bend beneath the big field.

Who could imagine that this place was formed by volcanic fire? And that the bare slopes, the sheer cliffs and uneven pasturelands were worn to the bone by the gouging and scraping of ice?

After the commotion of its creation, the cwm is a peaceful place nowadays, a vessel for silence. "Cwm Maesglasau is a small valley far from the merriment of mankind," observed J. Breese Davies. "The silence inclines a man to think he has left the ordinary world far behind and it comes as no surprise that religious hermits lived here once."

I too have lived in this valley's quietness all my life: the first half in its mouth, the second half in its tail; the first half with my family, *the second half without them. Cwm Maesglasau is my world. Its boundaries are my boundaries. To leave it will be unbearably painful. But this I know: when I move on, and when my remains are scattered on the land at Maesglasau, I will have given my life to the fulfilment of this valley's tranquillity.*

My obliteration will be its completion.

At Springtide, when the weather is more temperate, and
the earth begins to warm, and though a fine skin of snow
may sometimes fall, it will not last long, and though frost
may harden the ground overnight, it is seemly for the sun's
warmth to soften the day.

Hugh Jones, 1774

I see my mother beside her husband in the cart, a handsome
couple on their way to their new home at Tynybraich. They
have just left the chapel at Dinas Mawddwy, a small village in
Merioneth which lies between two mountain passes.

June's golden sun warms them. Behind them a wedding – and
the echo of wheel and hoof on road. Ahead of them a new life: the
pull of a mare towards a green and empty valley.

Evan has no need to prompt her; the mare turns left, instinc-
tively, off the turnpike road into a smaller lane. There is a crimson
tunnel of foxgloves and a sparkling dome of elderflower: the same

intricate design, Evan notices, as the lace on his wife's bodice. Sunshine streaming through the canopy spangles her hair with stars.

He puts an arm around her waist and draws her closer.

There is the mesmerising beat of hooves and the lingering smell of hawthorn. Gold and silver flowers shine from the hedge. They pass Ffridd Gulcwm without noticing the neighbours who wait to greet them, framed in the doorway. They pass the barn and go through the open gate.

The mare is slowed by the hill's sharp incline. But Evan is impatient; wanting to get home, he whispers a word, loosening the reins with a flick of his wrist.

Here, the road becomes uneven, the stream falling from Foel Dinas hindering them further. There is a panic of rabbits at each bend in the road; patterns of birdsong on the fringe of their consciousness.

And then – as the crunch of the wheel sharpens on the road's surface; as the heat increases suddenly; as a flash of sunshine blinds them – the newlyweds are flushed from their scented tunnel into the wide open valley of Maesglasau.

And here they are. Evan draws the reins. The mare comes to a halt at the top of the hill. The valley lies below them, around them, everywhere.

Tynybraich and the road to Cwm Maesglasau

This will be the vessel of their marriage. A valley between three mountains and a distant waterfall. The sheep and the cattle are black-and-white gems on a cushion of green grass. The old stone-built farmhouse at Tynybraich sits in the crook of the mountain.

I see my mother stirring, then steadying herself as she sits between her husband and the flank of the cart. My father turns to her. She smiles.

Encouraged, he flicks the reins. The mare trots faster, down-hill, over the bridge spanning the stream, and rising again up the slope of Tynybraich mountain to face the walls of married life.

It is a handsome house. Three centuries old, says Evan as he helps her from the cart. Two windows on each side of a big wooden door, with the three windows above creating triangles in the roof. On one side the *tŷ ffwrn*, an outhouse with an oven, where the bread is baked. On the other side a shippon and stable, encircling the farmyard. Smoke drifts from a chimney. A sign that Evan's family awaits them.

I imagine my mother bracing herself.

She is drawn by Evan through the oak door of Tynybraich, not towards the parlour on the right, nor the little room straight ahead. Their first duty is to step inside the large front room. Three women are sitting around the fire. Of the three, only two raise their expectant eyes to meet those of my mother. The third, the oldest, fixes her gaze on the hearthstone, dousing the fire with her cold stare.

These three were Evan's two sisters and his mother.

I imagine my mother averting her gaze to the dark oak furniture; the corner cupboard, the dresser, the grandfather clock, and the big red chest with iron clasps, where the family's treasured old books are kept.

One of the sisters rises and introduces herself. She is Sarah, who then walks to the kitchen to put the kettle on the fire.

The other is Annie. She approaches and kisses them both. The villagers had said that Annie was "not quite like everyone else". She'd wander around on her own, talking to trees and flowers. Rumour had it she'd eaten some poison from a hedge. No, said Evan, Annie had been different from birth.

Old Catrin Jones is still staring into the fireplace. She was known as a bit of a dragon, unlike her husband – God rest his soul – who'd been a gentle and astute man, fond of books and music.

What a pity Robert Jones wasn't still alive to temper his wife's scorn.

Her bridal dress digs into my mother's flesh. Tears prick her eyes. As she moves through the house, she recalls her own warm hearth at Coed Ladur: her parents, her brothers and sisters.

Evan ignores his mother's scowl. He pulls his wife after him, past the buttery with all its tackle, towards the back kitchen.

This is a warmer hearth. It has an oven and a griddle, and a black kettle hanging from a chain. It has a slate slab for baking and a smoothing iron. A peat fire smoulders behind a shiny brass fender, filling the room with its bittersweet aroma.

There is a long oak table with a settle, a bench, and two chairs at each end. Hanging from hooks in the low ceiling are a flitch of bacon, two jugs and two large pans. At the far end of the room: a cupboard full of white dishes, two rolling pins, a crook-backed flour caddy, a large earthenware bowl for the washing up, and then the back door opening onto the wide expanse of the valley.

Halfway through the wedding repast Evan's mother comes to join her children. She leaves her bread and butter half eaten; she picks at the fruit bread and the pancakes, and barely touches the milky tea though her mouth is parched.

She did not attend her son's wedding. Nor did she let her two daughters go. Why should she bless that which took everything away from her? Her only son? Her own home? Tradition demanded that she made way for Evan and his new wife. She would have to move from the farmhouse at Tynybraich to a smaller house at the far end of the cwm.

Her farewell is sulky too. And while Evan is joking with his sisters, she quietly hisses in her daughter-in-law's ear:

"We shan't get used to you around this place. The three of us used to get along like the three legs of a milking stool. Now you've come to change that."

I can see my mother staring at her. Her response is quiet:

"I've never quarrelled with anyone in my life, Catrin Jones, and I'm not going to start now."

As men come in waves to conquer new lands, so came three young women from three neighbouring valleys to inhabit the cwm at Maesglasau. My mother – Rebecca Jones from Cwm Cynllwyd –

was the last of three generations of women to cross the pass of Bwlch y Groes to live at the end of the world.

It was early Spring 1903 when she left her home near Llanuwchllyn to visit her relatives at Bwlch farm in Dinas Mawddwy. Crossing over the steep pass at Bwlch y Groes, little did she know she'd never return. She was carrying water from the well to the wash-house when a young man came to Bwlch. He was seeking a copy of *The Shepherd's Companion*, a handbook written by her grandfather listing the earmarks of sheep in the Mawddwy valley.

The young stranger was called Evan Jones of Tynybraich, and his heroic feats as farmer, hunter and mischief-maker were part of local lore.

Evan was a man of the land and of the open air, with none of his forebears' love of books. He was a good farmer – everyone said so – and he knew every sheep in his flock by name. As a poacher he was even better.

He could catch moles like nobody else. He'd hear the mole pass beneath his feet and reach into his waistcoat pocket. Placing a drop of poison onto a worm, he'd push the deadly morsel into the mole's path.

They said that Evan could catch trout by tickling their bellies. Standing still in the river, he'd stoop towards the water and wait until the fish was motionless. He'd lower his hands and encircle the fish. Tenderly he tickled the trout, transfixing it. Then – in a sudden sublime movement – he'd cast the trout out of the living, breathing water into deadly air.

Above all else, Evan was a hunter, though he never followed the pack, preferring to make his way alone to Bwlch y Siglen at Maesglasau. There he would stand and wait. It might be all day. For Evan Jones understood the fox. He knew with certainty that it would come sooner or later, crossing Bwlch y Siglen on the way to its lair.

Evan stood, listened, waited, and got his reward.

My mother fell in love with this handsome, skilful and plain-spoken man, with his large moustache and with mischief in his eyes. Three months later they were married.

The year 1905 was a year of death in the annals of the world. Czar Nicholas II slaughtered five thousand in the city of St Petersburg. Ten thousand were killed in an Indian earthquake. Two hundred thousand Russians were killed by Togo's Japanese navy. Sailors on the Russian ship Potemkin killed their own officers. Jews were killed by the Russians of Odessa. And in Wales, nearly a hundred-and-twenty miners died in a pit explosion in Rhondda Fach.

But for Rebecca and Evan Jones, Tynybraich, the birth of their first child was enough to counter all that death: an armful of flesh and a thatch of black hair. I was named Rebecca after my mother and grandmother. Tradition had a hold on me from the moment I was born.

Catrin Jones, my grandmother, never came for the birth, nor for some weeks later. She eventually came to bestow her curt blessing and declared me "bonny like my father". These were hard times for Mother. But Aunt Sarah lent her support, both at my birth and afterwards, Father only too glad to make his excuses and escape to the fields. Sarah continued to help with the housework and with bringing up "little Beca". And when my brother, Robert, was born in August 1906 she came to us every day, despite her mother's reproaches.

I have only a child's memory of Aunt Sarah. I remember her as a tall and handsome woman, serious and quiet, unlike her more mischievous brother. I remember how my mother's face would light up with a smile as she greeted her every morning; a smile of thankfulness; a sister's smile.

Sarah died in 1910, a young woman of thirty-four years, a year after the death of her own mother. What has stayed with me most is an impression of quiet gravity. Or maybe that impression comes from the short poem – an *englyn* – composed in her memory, which is carved into her gravestone on the hillside at Dinas Mawddwy:

> Early was Sara silenced – tranquil, serious,
>> She fell quiet ere the crowd's applause;
>> But the spell cast by her life's goodness
>> Radiates over her cold resting place.

Without her sister-in-law, my mother would have had to bring up two children on her own, as well as run the household and fulfil the many duties of a farmer's wife in a remote valley.

She'd rise at daybreak to rekindle the fire and polish the hearthstone with black lead and two brushes, after which she'd put whiting under the grate. She'd polish the fender with Brasso and use dock leaves to clean the stone floor, sweeping it thoroughly before we awoke. Then she'd cook breakfast and prepare lunch for midday.

After feeding and clothing her children she'd complete the rest of the housework. Monday was washing day. Mother would scrub the clothes and push them through the mangle, spreading them on the hedges to dry in the sun. On Tuesday she'd smoothe the clothes with the box iron, each iron being lifted white-hot off the fire. Wednesday was baking day, when enough bread was baked for the week (seven loaves), not counting two loaves of *bara brith* (fruit bread), and unleavened cakes. Thursday was butter-making day, which involved rotating the churn and patting the butter in the kneading-dish, before finally scrubbing the dairy clean. And

Friday was the day for house-cleaning; seldom could she go to market at Dolgellau.

In addition to all this Mother had her tasks on the farm. Carrying water from the well to the house. Feeding the hens and collecting eggs from the carthouse. Feeding the pigs and mucking out the sheds. She had to milk the three black cows in the cowshed and ensure that there was enough food for them in the mangers. And when Aunt Sarah was unavailable, it was Mother who'd walk all the way to Llidiart-y-Dŵr where she'd leave a pitcher of milk for her mother-in-law.

In the midst of all this she was expected to care for us children, to prepare meals and lay on tea punctually for my father when he came in from the mountain. He would arrive on the hour. It was no small matter to prepare meals with the little we had. For breakfast there was porridge. We'd have salted bacon and potatoes, or broth, for lunch, and then bread and butter with jam and buttermilk for supper. We ate fruit according to the season: rhubarb, plums, gooseberries, apples and blackberries (fondly known as "the poor man's fruit"). There would be a tart, and it was I who adorned its pastry lid with the salamander, a hot flatiron which produced a patterned golden crust.

Were it not for my father's hunting and fishing our supply of fresh meat would have been limited to the slaughter of a pig. Each farm would kill a pig in turn, with everyone sharing the fresh meat between them; anything left over was preserved with a mixture of salt and saltpetre. We could expect a steady supply of fresh meat for some five months of the year.

At important times, such as shearing or harvest, Mother was expected to do her share of the tasks, in addition to preparing food and drink for a horde of men twice in a day. After clearing the table she'd go out again to work until sunset. Then she'd need to prepare supper for everyone and put us children to bed, after which she'd clean the tens of plates and dishes that had accumulated during the day.

My father never offered to help. It wasn't expected.

When she did manage to snatch some rest in the evening her hands were still busy, knitting socks. It was my privilege, when I was old enough, to help her wind the wool in skeins around my upraised hands. The wool was bought from two brothers at Cwm Llinau.

When Mother wasn't knitting she would read. The Bible was the only book. She had decided at the age of fourteen to dedicate her life to Jesus.

Some time ago I discovered among Mother's old papers a short essay she wrote on the subject of Time. It reveals her dedication to her inner life, despite her outward industry.

This is part of what she wrote in that essay:

> At times it is enquired how man can cultivate his mind.
> This can be answered easily, that many carve out time
> through proper use of their idle moments. He who follows
> his work with a provident spirit will pursue the moment
> while caring for his duties at the same time.

My mother made the most of the few "idle moments" that came her way. Throughout her life she accepted life's cruel blows, incorporating them into her rich spiritual life, which glowed like a pearl within her and shone through the skin of her face. Her motto was "believe in God and do your work".

Robert soon became "Bob": my friend and playmate. We never stopped. We played with passion, and in harmony.

A large oak had been blasted onto its side by a lightning bolt. This was our home. The tree's enormous roots formed a solid gable, its many nooks and crannies our shelves and cupboards. Our domestic arrangements worked perfectly. Bob went hunting with his bow and arrow, returning a few minutes later with a piece of wood in his hand and a look of victory on his face. The wood had put up "a hell of a fight", said the little hunter. I laid out tea for my brother's homecoming; leaves and rain water in an old can. I had prepared mud cakes for him, with a topping of moss for green icing. They were baked to perfection in a crevice between two roots. Bob ate them to please me.

A rich aunt had given us an old cart. My father tied a box to its front, so that we could carry goods to Maesglasau or to Ffridd: eggs, or a jar of treacle, or a bottle of cold tea for my father. The greatest fun was to carry farm animals in the box. Bobby-Joe, the lamb, sat majestically on his four-wheeled throne, whereas Blodwen, the hen, clasped her talons onto the fore beam, her red wings flapping like an unruly windmill as she tried to keep her balance when we speeded downhill. We would laugh so much. Even Father, crossing a field, would stifle a smile.

Our stagecoach was the peat-sledge, the wooden contraption used to drag sods of peat from the uplands. We would delight in Father's return from the mountain, watching patiently and making sure we didn't get "under his feet" as he unloaded the peat with care: this was fuel for our fire. If Father was in a good mood, he'd invite us to step on the empty peat-sledge and ride around the yard, every cat and dog exhorted to come aboard, until the sledge was a travelling circus moving noisily through the farm.

At other times – fearful for our safety – he could be quite severe, and we were careful to keep out of his way. Our play was sweetest when out of sight, and Father's prohibitions were a great inducement. Thus we ventured to the ravine, to spy on the "den of foxes"; or climbed the steep side of Tynybraich mountain to hunt "the gang of bandits".

But despite his severity, Evan Jones was a fine story-teller, and his comic accounts of his own feats, and the unfortunate events which befell others, mesmerised us. His tales trumped the scriptural stories we heard from Mother at bedtime, each with some lesson we could always foresee.

I see her now still in her work clothes – an apron made from sacking and a tape clasping the waist – as she folded back the bedclothes and insisted we pray. We'd go on our knees and recite the words she had taught us:

> When rising at morn to the life that is due,
> Put your face into water to freshen your hue,
> And utter a prayer before tasting your fare,
> In case you get captured in Bel Ffego's snare.

Much to her consternation there would be quiet laughter, and we'd badger her as to the exact nature of "Bel Ffego". She would reproach us for our childish blasphemy. When she left we concocted sham prayers.

On Sabbath there was to be no playing nor drawing nor knitting nor sewing, nor indeed any other activity. Nothing but the weekly trip to chapel and Sunday school. But Bob and I became cunning. In an innocent voice we'd beg Mother's permission to go out and "stretch our legs". We would run to our hiding places, gaining a few minutes of freedom to play, to shout and to laugh. The forbidden play of the Sabbath was sweetest.

Our other escape was books. Bob and I had learned to read at school in Dinas Mawddwy and were now fervent readers. On the Sabbath we escaped to imaginary lands, and boredom was kept at bay. Mother subscribed to *Y Dysgedydd* (The Instructor), and we little ones received *Dysgedydd y Plant* (The Children's Instructor), and from this we learned simple poems on Biblical history such as this rhyme about Jesus Christ greeting his disciples:

> To find the best advantage,
> Aboard a boat he'd go,
> So everyone could hear him
> Quite clearly from the shore.

Father was no reader. I cannot remember him ever lifting a book or a pen. Mother dealt with what little paperwork the farm generated. She'd have to sit in the kitchen at the end of a long working day because Father insisted on some letter being written *now*. She'd phrase the letter with care, but Father scorned her sedate turn of phrase:

"They won't understand that, Beca. Just write: 'The sheep have arrived.' That's all that's needed."

"But Evan . . ."

"No more nonsense. Just what's needed, no more."

Father seldom showed any interest in the family's old books. In a way it was understandable. He'd had to work hard on the farm following the negligence of his own father who'd been more interested in books than sheep. I never saw Father undoing the iron clasps on the oxblood chest in which the old books were kept, nor reaching for the treasures within: a sixteenth-century book by William Salesbury; William Morgan's 1588 Bible; John Davies of Mallwyd's "Little" Bible of the seventeenth century; our copy of the 1742 Book of Common Prayer, not to mention the many early English books bought in London by our forefathers. It is this chest which is alluded to in the memorial *englyn* composed for our grandfather, Robert Jones:

> He was laden with literature – his chests
> Were castles of knowledge;
> While in search of the whole truth
> Learning's hot sun enlightened him.

Away from our parents' gaze, what a secret pleasure it was for us children to take those old, old books from the chest and wonder at the fragile pages.

The most exciting for us was the Book of Common Prayer, for

in faded yellow writing on a blank page someone had documented the family tree. It claimed that our family had lived at Tynybraich since 1012. We believed it, and committed to memory every name in the lineage, a catechism of males (except for the proverbial exception): "Gethin, Gruffydd, Llywelyn, Evan, Llywelyn, Elis, William, John Evan, Robert, Robert, Mary Evan, Evan, Robert and Evan Jones. Christ's Year 1012. These are they who owned Tynybraich."

The smallest book in the chest, *Kynniver Llith a Ban* by William Salesbury, was also a favourite, though the antiquated Welsh was sometimes hard to understand. We would stare in wonder at the Greek letters at the beginning of the book, the decorated capitals, the pattern of words on the page, and the two decorative hands at the end. There were notes in brown ink in the margin written by some old, old man.

Its opening words are imprinted on my memory, despite their strangeness:

Kynniver llith a ban or yscrythur lan ac a ðarlleir yr Eccleis pryd Commun / y Sulieu a'r Gwilieu trwy'r vlwydyn: o Cambereiciat W.S.

At the close of the Blessings at the end there was a reference to Jesus Christ sighting the multitude and ascending atop a mountain to speak unto them:

Pan welað Ieshu y minteioeð / e ðaeth i vyny i'r mynyth.

And we would imagine the son of God climbing the mountain at Maesglasau and standing there, amid the sheep, to address the people of Dinas Mawddwy.

We did not know that this was one of the first books to be printed in Welsh, published in London in 1551, and containing the first scriptural translations into Welsh from the original languages. *Kynniver Llith a Ban* was a very rare book. Only five copies remained.

We worked hard at school, both of us thirsty for knowledge. Much to Bob's annoyance, I was good at arithmetic, answering such questions as "How many pounds in 29 shillings?" or "1 yard of cloth will cost the purchaser 3 shillings. Find the value of 24 yards". But Bob excelled at logic, and coupled with the obstinacy of the Tynybraich family, it made him a first rate debater, even then. He would have made a fine barrister. But Bob wanted to become a doctor, I a nurse.

I still have some of my school books to this day, filled with the even handwriting that I envy today when I see the crabby, wavering scrawl of an old woman.

It was in these B. L. Exercise Books that I wrote my first compositions! We received most of our early education in English at Dinas Mawddwy; but at Sunday School all reading and writing was in Welsh. I see today a neat list (in English, of course) of the countries belonging to the British Empire, under the heading "British Possessions". I wonder if Cwm Maesglasau belonged there?

In English, too, I recorded the history of the "Cambrian Railway" and "King Alfred", together with a poem entitled "*Pro nobis*", and the following passage which describes the comings and goings during "My Christmas Holidays":

The school closed on December 23rd, 1915 and opened on January 11th, 1916, we had a fortnight's holidays. It was very wet throughout our holidays, but I enjoyed myself during them. The shops were full of toys and other things, they were trimmed with holly in the holidays. Christmas was on Saturday last year. I went to chapel in the morning and afternoon. Some people went away during the holidays and others came home.

Strangely enough, this is the only "memory" I have of Christmas as a child. And I no longer remember if this description was fact or fiction: to be sure, there weren't many "shops" at Dinas, though the reference to chapelgoing rings true.

There are rare examples of writing in Welsh in these books too, such as a page on "The Cow", and an essay on "The Blind Harpist". And a poem by Elfed, explaining to the little children of Dinas Mawddwy the difference between black and white:

"BLACK AND WHITE" (ELFED)

At the foot of the Alps in summertime
Two little brooks do flow,
One is called the white brook,
And the other is called the black.

From a sea of ice the white brook flows,
Its flood as white as milk;
Nor does it start its journey down
At any time but this.

The black brook starts another way,
With a blacker, blacker ice.
When winter makes this torrent freeze
The colour of the ice is black.

How vexing, every day on earth
To expose a truth like this –
It's easier changing white to black
Than turning black to white.

All poetry had to be learned off by heart, not to mention countless hymns and verses from the Bible. They remain in my memory to this day, echoes of a Welsh chapel childhood.

Our Sunday School teacher, John Baldwyn Jones, insisted we learn a poem by rote every week, not always Christian. He loved poetry (both Welsh and English), was a poet himself and the son of a poet: my grandfather's brother, a solid man with a long white beard who was known in bardic circles as J. J. Tynybraich.

Uncle Baldwyn was a great favourite among the children of the Sunday School. He'd been to university at Bangor where he'd excelled at hockey (of all things), and had also learned French. But home he came to help his father run his coal business, and to write about life in Cwm Mawddwy. He praised his native area's beauty as if he were praising God himself.

Here is my favourite *englyn* by him, which compares dreams to smoke rising from the "altar" of a pillow:

"THE PILLOW"

The pillow's a white altar – slowly
The day's late sacrifices smoulder,
And light smoke rises softly
As dreams to happy realms.

He was a frail man, but full of fun, and he loved the company of children and young people. He adored the Romantics – the poetry of Keats, Shelley, Tennyson and T. Gwynn Jones – and the novels of Daniel Owen. Indeed, he was compared once with the novelist's most famous character, the likeable and bubbly Wil Bryan.

Baldwyn translated poems from French to Welsh, he composed articles on Welsh literature and wrote stories, and also turned his hand to drama, portraying characters suffering social injustice in an almost "syndicalist" manner, according to one commentator.

However, his health was delicate. He did not go to fight in the Great War. But like so many of his peers, John Baldwyn Jones died during it, a young man of twenty-nine.

I have a volume of his poetry beside me, with an introduction by the great poet R. Williams Parry. There is a picture of Uncle Baldwyn, frozen by the eye of the camera. But his face is animated, as if he were in the middle of saying something.

Memories of my childhood reach me in a continuous flow: smells and tastes and sights converging in a surging current. And just like the stream at Maesglasau, these recollections are a product of the landscape in our part of rural mid-Wales at the beginning of the twentieth century. Its familiar bubbling comforts me.

It was not really like that, of course. The flow was halted frequently. Indeed a stream is not the best metaphor for life's irregular flow between one dam and the next.

I have not mentioned the reservoirs. In these the emotions congregate. I approach them with hesitation. I stare into the still waters, fearing their hold on my memories. In terror I see my own history in the bottomless depths.

Swimming against the current, I venture to the first dam. For this changed the course of our family life at Tynybraich.

I see my mother in bed with a baby in her arms. Father leans over her. The light of the candle shines on their faces, and on the dark beams of the big bedroom's ceiling.

I am three years old and I have climbed out of bed, seeking out my parents' voices. There is a cry. It comes from our new baby brother, Gruffydd.

Bob is still sleeping soundly.

I walk across the creaky floorboards and look through the gap in the door. Mother, Father and baby are caught in a halo of light. All I can hear is soft conversation. My parents' closeness unnerves me.

There is concern on their faces as they gaze down at my dark-haired brother who is but a few weeks old. I shiver in my nightdress.

I see Father take out a watch from his waistcoat pocket.

Grasping the chain, he allows the golden disc to swing to and fro in front of the baby's eyes. He checks the chain's motion. He clasps the watch in the palm of his hand before putting it away.

In a cracked voice, he says:

"I'm afraid, Beca, that the little boy can't see."

A silence. And I am paralysed, though my legs are shaking.

I hear my mother's voice. She raises her eyes to her husband's face:

"I'm not so sure, Evan. He'll be all right. You know he was early . . ."

Further silence.

I don't know how long I stand there, listening to the ticking of the grandfather clock down below in the hallway. In a while my mother's voice speaks again. It seems to come from far away.

"I'm afraid to say it Evan, but I think you may be right."

"No, come on now, it's too early for us to give up hope . . ."

I cannot remember turning away from their mutual comforting. Neither do I remember re-crossing the floorboards and returning to the bedroom. I cannot remember getting into bed again. But I remember turning to look at Bob, and with all the passion of a three-year-old, begrudging him his sleep.

And I remember lying there as the dam burst, and as the tears drowned me, because my baby brother, Gruffydd, had been born blind.

With the dignity and grace which characterised her whole life, my mother soon came to accept Gruff's blindness. Understandably, Father's reaction was one of anger and confusion. He wanted to know the cause of the blindness. He would not believe that "nothing could be done" to give sight to his son. He took the baby boy to a doctor near Aberystwyth, but left without aid or explanation. The doctor just confirmed that Gruffydd was blind for life.

In time our lives returned to normality. I played with my new brother: feeding him and playing mother, while Mother was working. I washed and dressed Gruff every day, with the help of Aunt Sarah, and he was a more willing plaything than Bob had ever been. At night he slept between his brother and big sister: three raven-haired heads under one white cover.

I helped him learn to walk, leading him carefully by the hand and showing him the way around the house and its furniture, avoiding the fireplace. I taught him new words and was thrilled when he repeated them. Gruff had a brighter and a sharper mind than any of us.

Bob had to go about his business on the farm while I completed these duties. As for the mud pies and the moss cakes, he did not once admit to missing them.

But then, Bob had always been proud.

*

In 1910, when I was five years old and Bob four, and Gruffydd just learning to walk and to count, we were told by Aunt Sarah that another baby brother had arrived. Bob huffed and inquired about his breakfast. My own response was to draw Gruff closer.

He was called William. The family at Tynybraich now numbered six.

Again I see my mother in her bed. The beams in the ceiling are low and dark. I see my father looking into the candle-flame with the eyes of a stunned man.

I push the door open and go to my mother. I sit beside her and open my arms to receive the little one, with all the maternal love of a five-year-old girl.

William was a healthy child with a round, pink face. He was a beautiful boy, with hair and lashes as black as night. But from the moment he was thrust into the light of this world, William, like his brother, was blind.

38

The stream begins her journey high on the crag above Maesglasau, rising from an underground seam up to the peaty uplands. Quietly, purposefully she flows to the edge of the precipice before plunging in a foamy, powerful waterfall hundreds of feet downwards. The water breaks into a hundred thousand shards in a rocky ravine, then falls towards the valley floor, over the still stones of the screefall, over jutting rocks and stone-strewn moraines, through them, past them and under them in a baptismal flood.

The bracken on the banks arcs towards her, our stream. The fox regards her from its den in the woods. The oak stands beside her. The rowan stoops over her. The hawthorn flees from her and the rushes tickle her.

Houses were positioned to make use of her.

But there's no stopping her now. The stream obeys the earth's primal forces, her silvery dance ceaseless, effervescent. How to separate the dancer from the dance, as a poet once said? How to separate the stream from the flow of her own water?

She passes the ruins of Tyddyn Uchaf, and the old house at Maesglasau Bach, where I live, and where the men raised a dam to form a dipping pool for the spring flocks. Today the stream flows unhindered through a breach in the wall, under a gate, past the ruin of Maesglasau, where swallows nest and sheep shelter from the rain and the sun. She avoids Llidiart y Dŵr and the remains of Tyddyn Berth, turning away, instead, by the cwm's fifth ruin and meandering towards the big field.

On the valley floor she flows below Bwlch y Siglen – the Pass of the Bog – reaching a spot where she once satisfied the demands of a lead mine, known as the quarry of the blue mark, with its "bottomless pit". Here she slows down in a flat furrow: the children would paddle here; men and women would wash their hands during haymaking. She's at her laziest here, a tranquil lagoon. The cows quench their thirst from her banks. The children ford her with slabs of stone. She glitters in the August sunshine, an oasis in the parched fields.

As the valley narrows the stream accelerates again, rushing along the boundary between the land of Tynybraich and Ffridd Gulcwm. Here, sunk below her banks, fishermen enter her to tickle the trout. She flows in the shadow of Foel Dinas, through the water turbine which has provided electricity for my family for half a century, under the bridge and on towards the old bungalow where my mother and William lived. And then, in an eternal and absolute marriage, she merges with another stream flowing from Cwm yr Eglwys.

She is never the same again, losing her name as she flows out of Cwm Maesglasau. At the base of the Oerddrws Pass she is doubly lost in the rout of the rivers Cerist and Dyfi.

She could not be blamed. How could she avoid the force of gravity? Every height contains a fall; descent is what the terrain demands of her.

Like the poet Taliesin she is a quicksilver creature, transforming herself countless times during her journey through the cwm.

But she has her moods, like all of us, and is transparent by nature. Never did I see a stream so responsive to time. When the first sunny rays of March arrive she's a maiden, a young madam, impulsive and cheeky in Spring, merciless on her flinty rockbed.

In June's warmth she can be febrile and delicate, licking the meandering banks with her tongue. During Autumn's tempests she's ruddy and tempestuous, breaching her banks. When December comes she's a recluse, her cataracts frozen into a hoary beard, yielding to nothing except a young adventurer's ice axe. A few seconds of thaw and he falls to oblivion. The emergency services arrive. A young body lies mangled in the ravine. In the flashing blue and red lights of the rescue vehicles, we listen to our midwinter murderess cackling coldly to herself.

She's never the same, the stream in Cwm Maesglasau, changing from one day to the next. Having lived with her throughout my life, and despite all her transformations, I know her more intimately than the blood in my own veins. When the stream's flow comes to an end, so will my own life.

Knowing this is what gives me peace.

2

Behold, the winter has waned, the rains have passed by and
are gone; the flowers of the earth are seen again, and the
birds are heard to sing: the light lingers longer every day
and the sun emerges oft from his tent above us in the
heavens; and there is nought that can hide from his heat.

Hugh Jones, 1774

There is a photograph, in faded black-and-white, showing the
family at Tynybraich in their Sunday best.

My father looks impatient, with an out-thrust elbow and restless feet. His coat pocket is bulging; his collar and tie are askew.
Iron nails are seen on the soles of his boots. He is a handsome
figure, standing there, his hand barely touching William's shoulder. There is sadness in his eyes, as though he were already sensing
the finality of that scene.

Lithe as a willow, my Mother leans towards her family. Her
kind eyes regard the camera with respectful distance. She is

wearing her dark dress, which accentuates her pale and flawless complexion. Her only adornments are her aunt's slim, gold brooch and her wedding ring. Her hair is swept back in a dark wave; her narrow waist and the acute angle of her elbow create a natural diamond. She cradles the head of her baby, William, gently turning it towards the unseen presence of the photographer.

William is a cherub of two, raised up between his parents, his face round and soft. He wears a new suit: its broad lace collar gives the impression of wings. His tiny hand clutches the hand of his father, his unseeing eyes turned away, as if some commotion elsewhere had captured his attention.

In front of him stands Gruffydd, also with a wing-like collar of lace. He, too, wears a dark suit with the substantial belt of a nobleman. His arms are held out and his eyes point downwards, fixed on a point of promise. Confidently – reassuringly – he grips the hands of his brother and sister; a last touch before leaving; a final lingering. His older brother's hand rests on his shoulder, as if attempting to hold him back; to defer his departure.

I see Bob rather as a smart squire in a new white-collared suit and a bow tie, waistcoat, and knickerbockers. His "best" shoes bear witness to scrabbling and climbing. His look is determined; his level gaze challenging the photographer's authority.

I stand in the narrow gap between my mother and my brothers, perched on the edge of a stool. My two feet are splayed

The Tynybraich family, c.1912 – Evan and Rebecca Jones, William (between his father and mother), Robert, Gruff and Rebecca

as I make room for my brother whilst attempting to keep my balance. Gruffydd's hand covers mine. My mother's left hand barely touches my shoulder. Hidden from sight, my brother William's hand grips my long tresses. Two bows of lace lie on either side of my head, like two dragonflies resting on my hair. I am wearing a new pinstripe frock with a starched collar and four silver buttons: *lady, baby, gypsy, queen* . . . And a cameo brooch passed down from my mother.

I was never so proud! My joy is evident. The excitement of the picture-taking shimmers in my eyes: the pomp of the setting; the camera's awesome technology; the miracle of the end-product.

I have that photograph in a frame by my bed. It was taken before Gruff was sent away to our relatives in London, to accustom him to noisy crowds and traffic.

He, this small boy from rural Wales, returned from the capital of England with his confidence intact, his independent nature having long since formed.

A year passes. My father is called upon to accompany his two sons to a preparatory school for blind children at Rhyl. Gruff is five, William three and a half.

At daybreak on a Saturday morning in 1913 we stand in an unfinished circle on the farmyard at Tynybraich. Gruff and William each have a bag slung across their shoulder containing essentials: a few clothes, socks, a parcel of food, a woollen scarf, a flannel, a piece of soap and a comb.

Mother kisses each son on the cheek. Bob shakes hands manfully. I kiss them too, before stepping back.

They climb into the cart and sit behind my father. Nestling against each other, they hold hands. They are allies now. My father does not utter a word. His mute back says it all.

He prompts the mare and the journey begins, across the farmyard and down along the mountain road, away from Tynybraich. Neither of the boys turns to look back as we stand there in our own darkness. Why should they, when seeing has always been a matter of feeling?

We stand in the early blueness of the day, watching the cart's departure. We are three grey idols, staring into the valley's great emptiness; staring at three other idols fading into the distance.

Finally, they vanish from sight. And at that moment we are blinded by the sun's first rays coming over Ffridd mountain, casting long shadows behind us.

I turn and run into the house, groping my way through hot tears up to my room. Through the window, down below, I catch a glimpse of my mother, still staring in front of her, as if trying to comprehend the breaking of day.

I cannot begin to understand what my parents went through at that time. There were no welfare benefits, no social workers, no advice for the "disabled" and their families. Rebecca and Evan Jones, Tynybraich, were given to understand that the only way they could educate their two blind sons was by sending them away to a special school. They saved what little money they had to pay for that education. We lived on virtually nothing for years.

In my hand now I have a shrivelled invoice bearing the following words:

> Received from Evan Jones Esq. of Dinas Mawddwy the sum of £5 for education of little boys.

My mother showed great courage in sending her blind sons away at such an early age. If faith could cure everyone, as it cured Bartimaeus son of Timaeus, then the sons of Rebecca Jones of Tynybraich would have had their sight.

Gruffydd and William's journey towards education would be irreversible, taking them away from the Welsh language and its culture to another language and culture; away from Wales to another country. We would not see them again until that process was well advanced.

When he returned from Rhyl two days later, my father did not speak about his two infant sons. I think that the pain of that parting stayed with him for ever.

The preparatory school at Rhyl was a homely and welcoming establishment, run by two sisters. But from there Gruffydd and

William went to another school in Liverpool. Here they complained that "the classes were cold, the food bad and the people worse." In their teens, they went to England's deepest interior, to Worcester and its College for the Blind: a school for blind boys modelled on the English public school.

There they learned the virtues of hierarchy, discipline and independence. They learned the meaning of words such as "fellow" and "master" and "prep". They learned about classical music, about the richness of European literature, about the glorious history of English kings and queens. They learned how to play chess and how to play the piano. They learned about cricket and football. And they learned about the chill of the dorm.

They learned the value of toughness, and the price of being homesick. They learned to live without a family; without the embrace of a mother and the word of a father; without the care of brother and sister.

They learned to worship in the Anglican way. And they learned how to talk with God – and with each other – in the formal English of the day.

Three times every year they came home to Tynybraich: a month at Christmas, a month at Easter and two months in the summer. They were welcomed back like prodigal sons.

They would hold hands, as if each was a white stick to the other on that uneven path between school and home. Those four months, a third of the year, were enough for them to keep their Welsh, and, I think, to reconcile them with their Welshness.

After sacrificing so much to send the boys to school, the means were simply not there to send myself and Bob to the County School. Our formal education ended at the village school. Then we returned to Cwm Maesglasau to earn our keep.

At the age of eleven Bob's dream of becoming a doctor ended, and he became an unwilling farmer.

As for me, I lifted the wooden casing off the old Singer sewing machine which I'd inherited from my Aunt Sarah, and started my "career" as a seamstress: responding to requests for a dress or a suit, for repairs and alterations, or to render an adult's clothes suitable for a child. And I enjoyed the handwork; it provided me with the busy stillness in which I could think.

Bob and I continued to read extensively, and we both made an effort – under the guidance of a representative of the Royal National Institute for the Blind – to learn how to decipher braille.

This marvellous system uses a system of six raised dots, with sixty-three possible permutations. Since Bob and I were still young, and since manual work hadn't yet coarsened our skin, the flesh on our fingers was still soft enough. I made sure I used a thimble when sewing, in order to protect the all-important index finger.

So it wasn't long before we'd both mastered our third language;

or at least we knew enough to read our brothers' letters.

In his teens, Gruff learned to type on a conventional type-writer so that Mother could read his letters. Thus she learned for herself about her sons' lives at school; a life which, even after a decade, remained as foreign to her as ever.

A fourth brother, sighted, was born at Tynybraich in 1917.

Like the rest of us, Ieuan was of dark complexion. I was allowed to care for the little one often, since my sewing work kept me indoors, while Mother was kept busy. In the absence of Gruffydd and William, here was a new baby I could care for. Ieuan grew into a sharp and lively child, full of laughter. He said his first word at a young age, and that word was *golau*: light. He learned to read and write, but his favourite activity was drawing. He would draw with his slate pen on his slate all day, portraying life at Tynybraich.

Bob and my father would grumble whenever Ieuan "got underfoot". There was no point explaining that the artist was merely following his muse.

Nothing pleased Ieuan more than walking to Maesglasau, where he'd draw a picture of the foaming waterfall as it shattered on the rock face, and the sad ruins of Maesglasau Mawr, with ferns growing through the windows and nettles in the hearth.

He often asked about his brothers, far from home, at school.

He would look intensely at Gruff and William when they returned home. Ieuan could not imagine what it was like to live without being able to see.

As if the keenness and power of both his brothers' eyes had accumulated in him, Ieuan's world was a place where seeing was everything.

Ieuan was three when Olwen was born – a sixth child for the Tynybraich family! Our cup was overflowing! Ieuan, no longer the baby, was more than happy. I too delighted in her. What was fifteen years between sister and sister?

I sewed together a gift for our new baby: a rag doll with golden hair and blue eyes, a patterned frock and ribbons in her hair. Olwen was little more than a dark-haired, black-eyed doll herself.

Ieuan drew a picture of her sleeping, feeding, crying. He drew a picture of Mother rocking the cradle. He drew a picture of my father, looming tall, looking down at his baby daughter.

My own thoughts wandered to the time when we could play together; talk together; share secrets; read together, sew and cook together. We could be true friends, as Mother and Aunt Sarah had been.

But such thoughts were in vain.

Olwen Mai died when she was two weeks old. Born in May. Dead in May. Even the bluebells lasted longer.

To this day I can remember her as she lay, still and pallid, in my mother's arms. Stunned, we stared at her face, her small nose, the perfect tiny fingers, and the dark eyes which never really had a chance to see.

A coffin was made to hold her which was shorter than an arm's length.

She had not been baptised, so the wise men of the chapel did not allow us to bury her by day. One fervent elder said she would surely go to Hell. We were made to wait until sunset before we could take little Olwen to the graveyard. She who had seen so little light of day was buried in the dark.

My father never again went to chapel. It was only out of respect for my mother that I did. I could only marvel at Mother's implacable faith. Not once did she show a sign of bitterness or self-pity.

It was the presence of little Ieuan, not the absence of Jesus Christ, that prevented me from darkening my vision of the world. But even that was taken away from me by the "Heavenly King", in whose righteousness my mother placed her faith.

I was telling Ieuan a story about the Gwylliaid Cochion, the Red Bandits of Dugoed, one evening: a chapter from our increasingly fanciful epic. (Ieuan had started to believe he could hear them tapping his window at night, seeking help to hoodwink the Baron.)

But that night he seemed not to listen. His eyes were glazed, his cheeks flushed. I raised my hand to his forehead and felt his fever. I hurried downstairs to tell Mother. She brought him some broth, but he would not drink.

Ieuan weakened during the days that followed. We tried every way to draw the heat from his body, to bring a smile to his pale face. The doctor recommended wrapping him in woollen blankets and placing him in front of a blazing fire, to sweat out the fever.

His condition deteriorated dramatically one night. His high temperature became a terrible fever. He shivered and sweated at the same time, and his face took on the pallor of a ghost. And he was slowly choking.

My father departed by moonlight to fetch the doctor. Eventually he found him in the Red Lion tavern. Grudgingly, the doctor left his seat.

I remember the doctor's arrival, tripping as he crossed the threshold. He was unsteady on his feet; his speech was blurred. He did not hold much hope, but judged it opportune to cut a hole in Ieuan's throat: a last ditch attempt to counter the boy's diphtheria. Whatever his intentions, he failed.

As dawn broke Ieuan turned to look at us, as if he wished us to be his last sight. I remember Father turning away.

Ieuan, the little artist, died on his fifth birthday.

*

The two brothers from Cwm Maesglasau made good progress at the Worcester College for the Blind. Towards the end of his time there, as he approached the age of eighteen, Gruffydd decided to become a chapel minister. He applied for a place at Bala-Bangor Theological College. He mentioned his early upbringing at Tynybraich, the family faith, his education at Worcester, his many qualifications and his blindness. The Congregationalists wrote back by return of post rejecting him.

His excellent results at school ensured him a place to read History at Bristol University. There, under the guidance of one of the History lecturers, he began not only to row, but also to box, in order to strengthen his weak lungs. He rowed, boxed and studied, and through his typical perseverance succeeded.

After graduating in 1933 he gained a place at Oxford to read Theology. He had set his sights on becoming an Anglican vicar. This was a happy period for him. We gained the impression, from his letters, that he was enjoying every minute of it, coping well with life in the "city of dreaming spires".

Gruffydd enjoyed his studies. He was by nature a man who enjoyed order, and formal, purposeful conversation.

The "gentlemanly" atmosphere at Mansfield College, Oxford was an extension of life at his school in Worcester. There were firm boundaries, not only spatial, but social and educational too. The enclosed quads and the neat gardens; the self-contained nature of the colleges. There was a daily routine, almost monastic, in which he and his companions shared breakfast, dinner and tea in the high-ceilinged college hall. All dressed in their black gowns, with Grace intoned in Latin before each meal. Even the terms – Michaelmas, Trinity, Hilary – were well-defined, each one exactly eight weeks long.

To this life there was regularity, discipline and hierarchy. Gruff enjoyed tutorials in the masters' panelled rooms, Sunday services at church and the junior common room's raucous meetings, as well as rugby, cricket, rowing and athletics.

It was at Oxford that he first came into contact with peers from Wales. Indeed, a Welsh-language service was held at Mansfield College every Sunday morning, which many of the Welsh students attended. Gruff was already too "British" to attend the meetings of Oxford's newly established branch of Plaid Cymru. But he enrolled immediately with the Dafydd ap Gwilym Society for the Oxford Welsh, the university's second oldest society, established by men of distinction at the end of the nineteenth century: luminaries such as Sir John Rhys, W. J. Gruffydd, and Sir John Morris-Jones.

Gruffydd wrote to us about "the Dafydd", as this society dedicated to a great fourteenth-century poet was called, noting its fiftieth anniversary whilst he himself was at Oxford. Indeed, Gruff was elected to the post of "arch-incense-bearer" – a key position in the society's secretive ceremonies. An Eisteddfod was held for members once a year, and Gruff won the competition for composing a limerick, the pinnacle of his literary career.

One of the highlights of the year for the young men of "the Dafydd" was to go in punts along the River Cherwell, followed by a meal at the Cherwell Arms. Gruff also wrote of his friends at the society, a number of them becoming distinguished and well-known figures in Wales, including the politician and nationalist, Gwynfor Evans; the philosopher, J. R. Jones; the novelist, Pennar Davies; and the historian, Hywel D. Lewis.

These were, of course, all men. My impression was that women did not really figure in life at Oxford. Though there were a significant number of female undergraduates at Oxford in the 1930s, they played a marginal role in university life, as far as I could see, and were rather disregarded by their male colleagues. Women were not allowed to be members of the Dafydd ap Gwilym Society at that time – a fact which did not change until the 1960s.

My impression was fortified when I went to Oxford with Bob. After reading about it, it was exciting to go there by train, to visit our brother and his college. I was not disappointed by the university's splendid architecture: the Bodley Library, the Radcliffe Camera Library and the circular Sheldonian theatre designed by Christopher Wren. The colleges seemed to be built with stones of gold, blazing against a bright blue sky when caught in the early morning sun. I listened in amazement to the chatter of students in the streets; stared at the countless bicycles wheeling through the city.

It was a great pity that Gruffydd could not see the outward beauty of his university.

But neither was I allowed to see within those golden walls. As a woman I was forbidden from viewing what lay behind them, and had to rely on the no-nonsense descriptions provided by Bob.

I felt disappointed and frustrated by this. In the words of Virginia Woolf, when she was chased off the lawn of an Oxbridge college by a Beadle: "This was the turf; there was the path. Only the Fellows and Scholars are allowed here; the gravel is the place for me."

After leaving Oxford, Gruffydd was ordained at Southwark Cathedral in London in 1937, and became vicar at Kennington. He stayed in London throughout the turbulent first years of the Second World War. As he approached his church one Sunday morning he was given to understand that the church had been destroyed by a bomb. His family at Tynybraich were worried about him, and finally he left London for the Welsh Marches in 1942, when he was given a living at Presteigne by the Bishop of Hereford.

Soon it was time for him to baptise his first child. Such was his nervousness that he held the infant upside-down and began to baptise his feet instead of his forehead. From the congregation came a cry: "It's the other end!" Gruff had to baptise the child a second time; he secretly believed that he'd apportioned that child a double measure of grace.

It was at Presteigne that he met Christine, whom he married in 1946. They had three children: Richard, Elizabeth and Hugh.

During the same year as his marriage Gruffydd was given the living of two churches in the villages of Little Marcle and Preston in Herefordshire. He remained their minister for the rest of his life.

This was a rich and fertile hop-growing area. Other crops, too, grew in abundance. Bob and his friends from Dinas Mawddwy would make the trip there to pick apples each harvest. Those excursions were greatly enjoyed. We were greatly in awe when they returned, laden with those Marcher apples, the fruits of Eden, providing such sweet sustenance during the cold winters in Cwm Maesglasau.

Whenever Gruff returned to Tynybraich he would be ushered into the parlour by Mother. In her eyes the formal parlour was more in keeping with his standing as a clergyman.

Bob was not so fearfully respectful. He and Gruff would have frequent debates. After all, one was a Labourite and the other a Tory. One was a Union man and the other an Establishment man. One a Welsh Congregationalist and the other an Anglican. Arguments were unavoidable, but rarely lasted long.

Bob always had some wry story to illustrate the corruption of the established church. One of them concerned a former cleric at Mallwyd who offered to reward his flock in the world to come. In order to make their mouths water with hunger – and they were literally famished, said Bob – he promised them "a very big dumpling, yes a huge dumpling – bigger even than the field of Cae Poeth". Bob would laugh as he recited this story, finding it hard to deliver the punchline.

Faced with his brother's scorn, Gruff maintained that by returning to the established church he had merely reactivated the pre-Revival religion of the Tynybraich family.

This thought seemed to comfort him.

As a curate, he came to preach at Mallwyd church. The congregation at the great scholar John Davies' old church were rather surprised to see that Tynybraich's frail little boy had grown into a solid man who read clearly and confidently from his braille Bible. And his English was the King's English.

Gruff's Welsh, too, was formal, his conversation dotted with phrases from William Morgan's Bible. Indeed, it's likely that "the great book" was responsible for keeping his Welsh alive. After all, he'd left Tynybraich for London at the age of three and a half, and had never properly returned.

William came home to live at Tynybraich after leaving school and began a career copying R.N.I.B. texts in braille. At last we had an opportunity to get to know our brother properly. Mother took great delight in caring for him. And William, now eighteen, could enjoy the maternal affection he had missed for almost fifteen years.

It wasn't easy for him to embrace life on the farm again. He brought elements of his public school education at Worcester with him to Tynybraich. This helped him to acclimatise. He would insist on doing physical exercise daily, walking from the farmyard at Tynybraich to Llidiart y Dŵr, and then back again. He'd walk to and fro for hours between lunch and tea. Like a pilgrim on some unknowable journey, he followed his path with a sense of purpose, turning on his heel at the same spot – to the inch – every time.

We had to be careful what we did along the road to Maesglasau, lest we disturb William as he did his exercises. Woe betide anyone who left an obstacle in his way. He would lose his temper, repeating his favourite expletive – *botheration!* – as if reciting a cross prayer. The pride he had inherited from Father, combined with Mother's devoutness, made every fall a cruel humiliation.

In fact, we gained two brothers at Tynybraich at that time. In 1927, a year before William returned, another son was born, the last child of Rebecca and Evan Jones as they approached the age of fifty. I myself was twenty-two when Lewis arrived, old enough to be his mother.

Lewis could see. He saw the greenness of the fields at Maesglasau. He saw the stream flowing through it. He saw the colours of the flowers in the hedges, and the changing hues of the trees. He saw the sun and the moon. He saw day and night.

But his eyesight was weak – and getting weaker.

Like Ieuan before him, Lewis loved to walk to Maesglasau. I would accompany him (for Mother disliked the cwm's narrow end, and its oppressive rock face). I revelled in my brother's company, thoughtful and articulate little Lewis, with his thick spectacles. Of all the children born at Tynybraich, we were the ones who looked most like each other. I believe we shared the same creative nature, and the same urge towards spirituality.

Lewis liked walking to Maesglasau alone, too, much to Mother's concern. He liked to sit on the banks of the stream, throwing stones, hearing them hit the water, noting how the sound changed with every throw. He'd sit by the ruin of Maesglasau Mawr imagining the monks communing with God to the sound of the stream. He'd sit on a ledge above it, listening to the haunting cry of the curlew, a sound that, for him, embodied the cwm. Yet, when he heard the bird's call he'd run away from Maesglasau towards his home at Tynybraich.

But there was no halting the deterioration in his eyesight. The time came when he too had to be sent away to school.

One Saturday morning in late May, Lewis disappeared. There was no trace of him. We called and searched the cwm, and eventually found him on a ledge above the house. He was lying face down among the bluebells. He had been crying.

I lay by his side, asking him what was wrong. He pressed the flowers against his eyes, inhaling their blue scent. He said that this was his last chance to see the bluebells. Next year he'd be at school, and his sight would go.

Lewis was six when he faced that. Through a veil of blue on the side of Tynybraich mountain he stared blindness in the face, and saw blue turn to grey.

By the time Lewis left Worcester College he was a masterful piano player and an excellent player of chess. He was steeped in the language and literature of France, was a lover of poetry and of the music of Bach. He went on to read Law at university in Aberystwyth, but left prematurely and went to Bala-Bangor College to study theology, a path which had been closed to his brother.

It wasn't long before his fellow students noticed his dry wit and his ability to take a ribbing. During a meeting in the common room one of his peers proposed that Lewis be appointed "chief rat catcher" at the college. This prompted great laughter. But Lewis took the wind from his sails:

"No problem," he responded. "I'll catch every rat I see."

He met Rachel when he went to work as a telephonist at the Ministry of Labour at Nottingham. They married and settled in that city, and had three children: Isobel, Bronwen and Dominic.

Lewis became a computer programmer at Nottingham University. And in the same way as he'd grown accustomed to the hills of his native cwm, he soon learned to cope with life in a busy city, with its constant stream of traffic, uneven pavements and impatient commuters.

Once, he'd been standing at a bus stop waiting to go to the city centre. Hearing the approaching bus, he stuck out his white stick to halt the vehicle.

The driver promptly told his blind customer he'd stopped the wrong bus – "You need the green bus, mate" – then drove on.

It was the clamour of the city which disturbed him most. He used to say that he closed his ears in Nottingham and didn't open them again until he was back at Tynybraich. As soon as he reached home he allowed his hearing to rejoin him, revelling in the sounds of the birds and the stream.

He came home often. Sharing the company of such a lovable, agreeable person was a joy to me. And it was a joy to my mother

Maesglasau stream

also, being able to call "Lew Bach" back to the nest again – the last of her brood.

It was Bob and I who'd fetch him home from the train at Cemaes Road, driving the familiar roads towards home. Supper would be on the table ready for him; he'd sit down to the same feast every time: two boiled eggs, with Mother seated in front of him spooning the egg into his mouth. Lewis would sit still and accept the soft food.

This rite – Lewis' first supper – was Mother's way of welcoming her favourite back to her.

Lewis would wander around the cwm as though his blindness did not hinder him. He'd go to Dinas Mawddwy to meet up with friends; he'd visit Dolgellau fair, and the annual August show. He'd go for jaunts on the back of Idris Puw's motorbike, or to play chess with Morris Roberts, the parson at Mallwyd, who was always amazed that Lewis could leave a game of chess half-finished and return to it a week later, still remembering the position of every piece on the board.

Lewis' defective eyesight had strengthened his memory.

Yet, it would be wrong to claim that Lewis came to terms with his blindness. He would have given anything to see Tyny-braich mountain again, and the faces of his family. Indeed, of the three brothers, Lewis was perhaps least reconciled to his blindness. The wish to see was a driving force in his life. His memory of colour was always awakened by the scents of Maesglasau.

His favourite pastime was seeing through the eyes of others. He loved listening to visual descriptions: evocations of landscapes; the description of a face, or a painting. Using his memory of colour he'd imagine the sights for himself.

I remember well sitting by his side one day at Tynybraich, and he said to me: "Tell me what you can see."

Unthinkingly, I looked around and said "nothing". I immediately realised my error and hastened to describe the scene around me.

Lewis also loved to compare two different descriptions of the same object. He would note how the descriptions varied; the differences of emphasis. He used his friends' and family's eyesight to get to know the world.

As for me, I was as happy to chat with Lewis at Tynybraich as Bob and Gruff were to argue and then make peace. We'd talk until the small hours, his face aglow in the soft glow of the embers. We'd talk about literature, art, religion.

It was during one of these conversations that Lewis mentioned his wish to convert to Catholicism. Despite his deep feelings towards non-conformism – the Sunday School, its congregational singing, its close ties with his upbringing and with Welshness in general – he yearned for an unshakeable dogma, something he felt was lacking in chapel religion.

Breaking the news to the family was difficult. Bob's response was silence, though I know he thought long and hard about his brother's decision. Mother could appreciate the Catholics' devotion to the Virgin Mary, but there were other aspects of their creed which greatly perplexed her. And yet, she said to me many times: "We all go to the same place in the end." Mother had a gentle way of ordering life.

Today, Lewis is an artist – a blind painter. When he retired he began to attend art classes, going by train from Nottingham to Leicester every week to receive training from a lady called Rachel Sullivan who specialised in teaching blind people to paint.

It is a remarkable art form. As with painting for sighted people, it involves the use of colours and markings on canvas. But the outcome – a visual product – is never seen by its creator.

Yet, who understands the meaning of colour better than Lewis?

On the blind painter's canvas every mark has its meaning: sad marks, angry marks, happy marks, dreamy marks. The meaning of each mark is conveyed by the slant of the brush. The union of markings and colours creates a powerful and unique means of expression.

Lewis is often inspired by poetry – a sonnet by Shakespeare, a poem by Shelley or Keats, or the poetry of his compatriots Dylan Thomas and R .S. Thomas. Each of his paintings is a representation of the emotions evoked by the poems.

For example, lines from a poem by William Blake inspired him to paint a bird of paradise flying from East to West, and there is also a field of flowers, and the figure of the poet, John Clare. An arm extends towards the bird, trying to grasp it. In the north of the picture there is a representation of the industrial revolution, conveying Nottingham.

> *He who binds to himself a joy*
> *Doth the winged life destroy.*

A few years ago Lewis won a European prize for one of his paintings. He travelled to Luxembourg to receive his prize and exhibit his picture. It was a self-portrait, an abstract expression of his relationship with the world.

On one side of the painting is a pattern drawn with the fingers. This is an expression of feeling and touch, representing the way Lewis, a blind man, interacts with the world. On the other side of the painting is an impression of a mountain, with a river flowing down its flank. On the banks of this river Lewis himself is represented, touching a stone from the ruin at Maesglasau, preparing to hurl it into the stream, so that he can hear its sound as it hits the water. An orange sun shines in the sky, just as Lewis remembers it. Not far from the sun hovers a dark cloud.

Lewis was surprised to receive the prize. Smiling in disbelief, with his usual wit, he could fully appreciate the irony of a blind man gaining glory in the field of visual art.

But I know that like Ieuan before him, Lewis loves painting. There came a second sight in the wake of his blindness.

There was a time when I cast my eyes further than the stream and the beautiful cwm she waters. I looked beyond the hedges and the primroses, buttercups, celandines, wood anemones, herb robert, pignut, pennywort, yellow toadflax, harebells, yarrow, foxgloves, red campion, vetches and knapweed. I looked beyond the small flowers of the field, beyond the hawthorn and blackthorn, and the wild rose. Beyond the swallow's nest in the ancient beams of the old house. Beyond the red berries of the rowan and the black berries of the elder. Beyond the hazelnuts and the acorns and the topmost branches of the trees.

It was at those times that I lifted my eyes to the hinterland above the high crag at Maesglasau.

And though I see it nowadays only in the mind's eye, it is not diminished. A quarter of a century has elapsed since I last climbed up there. I must content myself now with life within the cwm. But before old age overcame me I climbed that crag countless times, sometimes for pleasure, but mainly to work. A thousand feet of Silurian cliff-face.

My brother Bob and I would make the ascent often enough. Sometimes it was in order to rescue a sheep gone astray, when we'd *have to lower ourselves on a rope onto a narrow rockshelf. At other times we'd climb up to the high pastures to count the lambs, to protect them from the fox or the cruel-beaked crow.*

In Winter's long months we'd ascend to seek out sheep in the snow, delving into the drifts with long poles. It would dishearten us to discover the frozen bodies. When a late snowfall occurred we found lambs whose mothers had lain on them, suffocating their own offspring.

Forasmuch as the Winter is a season of tempests, and the elements do conspire against all life, and bring upon the land great hardship, and losses are manifold, most specially with sheep, which are forbade to crop the sustenance of the sweet grass when the snow hath overcome the land, and they shall be covered over, bye the bye, underneath the drifts.

Hugh Jones, 1774

As Winter loosened its cold grip we'd climb the mountain again, this time to drive the sheep down to the farm's lowland meadows, so that they could be docked, washed, sheared and marked with pitch. We'd start our trek in the small hours, as the sky took on shades of blue, pink, yellow and white, and the night's bruise was on the mend.

The thrill of those heights never lost its magic. As we ascended, different shades of green gave way to the peat bog's sombre tones and the darkness of ancient oak woods. The marshland extended in one direction as far as Dyfi Forest and the heights of Aberangell and Mallwyd; in the other it stretched to Gribin Fawr and Gribin Fach, then onwards to the vale of Llyn Mwyngil. Here was lonely moorland unevenly spread, like a huge rumpled blanket, decorated with bell heather and bilberry, cotton grass sticking out like duck down.

At last, having reached Craig Rhiw Erch, I could pause to get my breath, facing the mountain peaks: Waun Oer, Foel y Ffridd, Foel Bendin, Glasgwm, Mynydd Ceiswyn, Mynydd Gwengraig and Cadair Idris. But I never ventured to the summit of the Cadair. It was said you'd come down mad – or a poet.

3

The season of harvest-tide, if we heed the opinion and
testimony of the wise, was also that happy time of year
when God created the earth . . . It is when He made a feast
for the whole world, and laid his table with sundry
sumptuous treats to fill his creatures with fine foods and
good cheer, they that wait upon him for all due sustenance,
in the allotted time.

Hugh Jones, 1774

The days of harvest were days of gold, rich and opulent. The green
gold of hay in swathes. The gold of haycock, rick and stack. The
gold of hayloft and barn. The gold of stubble.

This was Rumpelstiltskin's gift of spinning straw into gold.

But it was no fairy tale: harvest time on the farm was the
busiest time of the year. A time to pray, asking Providence for
protection against the rain.

We had wet harvests, certainly, with rain weeping on the fields.

74

But as I recall those golden times, the memory of sun dries up the tears.

A day was chosen (rain discounted), and a procession of men would wind its way to the fields, each carrying a scythe which swayed with each step. The grass was mown in silence, the blades moving steadily in unison. *Lladd gwair*, "killing" the summer hay, was an act of quiet intensity.

Once mown, the hay was left to dry in the sun, ranked in neat swathes. The upper side was left for a day or two, then Mother and I raked each row over, in order to get the full benefit of the sun. It was a gift we had: hooking our rakes under the swathe, flicking the wrist and tossing the hay so that it landed upside down in the same spot. The reverse side, too, was left to dry for a day or so.

The next step was to spread the hay, working our way through the field, dispersing the damp clumps. The crop had to be dried through, otherwise it would turn mouldy, giving our animals' winter fodder a bitter taste.

After it had dried, the hay had to be gathered. This, for me, was the heart of the harvest. All the farmsteads in Dinas Mawddwy came together to complete the task. Everyone pitched in, moving from one farm to the next by rote. A dozen, fifteen, twenty farmers worked shoulder to shoulder with a common aim.

It was hard work. The slightest indication of rain was like a whip driving a slave into action. The swathes were gathered into tussocks, smallish mounds of hay rounded in such a way as to repel the worst of any rainfall. The name for fair-weather stacks was *heulogod*. Using pitchforks we would carry these to a big haystack at the bottom of the field. Each haystack in turn was carried towards hayloft and barn in the cart.

The children's task was to climb aboard the heaped-up cart to tread down the hay. I remember leaping up, then throwing myself into the warm, springy prickliness of dead grass. Between the peppery aroma of dry hay and the crystal-clear waters of the stream, harvest time delighted our wide-awake senses.

Getting the hay into the barn was a great relief, guaranteeing food for the animals for the long winter. This sense of relief belongs to the past. We no longer experience it with the arrival of the big-bales' polythene shrouds.

What I revelled in more than anything during those days of harvest was the break between each burst of activity (though it wasn't much of a rest for us women). We'd have to leave the field to fetch tea to quench the men's thirst. Everyone sat around an old tree stump on the riverbank, waiting for refreshment. It was a time of great conviviality as everyone chatted and teased, listened to a story or fell into a reverie. Four o'clock was teatime in the fields: bread and butter with damson jam, pancakes made with buttermilk; a loaf or two of bara brith. The men would eat it all, hardly noticing what or how much they ate after toiling in the fields.

At lunch and supper everyone returned to the house and gathered around the table in the kitchen, ready for the food prepared for them by Mother and myself. In no time at all, the ravenous men devoured the meat and potatoes, followed by rice pudding.

Soon after harvesting the hay came the time to harvest corn. The same skill was called for. The corn was cut with a scythe and gathered into sheaves, then tied together with straw. The sheaves were brought together in fours to form stooks. The fields of stooks in those Indian summers, standing in still rows, drying in the heat, were a marvellous sight. They were proof of our labour. As soon as they were dry they were transported by cart to the barn. It was here that threshing took place, the ears of corn separated from the straw. Then the yield was winnowed to separate the grain from the chaff.

In the old days the grain would be taken to the nearest mill to be ground into flour, although my own memories stretch no further than seeing the grain stored in sacks, to be used as cattle-feed throughout the winter. The straw was chopped up finely and carried in sacks as a supplement feed for the cattle. Thus, all the goodness of the crop was used.

In the autumn, the russet-coloured bracken was cut and carried in armfuls to the barn, to be used as winter bedding for the cattle. I recall its aroma: a harsh smell, pungent and sharp.

The harvest demanded much from the shire horse which drew

the haywain, as it had drawn the plough in spring. I remember two horses from those distant days. One was named Robin: a bad-tempered blue-grey horse which bit me. The other was Captain, white and good-natured. Indeed, Captain and I became the best of friends. I was allowed to climb up onto his broad back and he'd carry me regally around the fields . . . until Father came.

The tractor did not arrive until after the Second World War, and a certain innocence was lost when the wheels of the Massey-Ferguson replaced the slow tramp of horses' hooves. But the iron horse was not sure-footed on the valley's many slopes. How many times did it career down the mountain, ripping away the mountain face? Bob managed each time to stay on, pressed inside the rolling ball of metal until it crashed upon the valley floor.

If I loved harvest, then Bob loved shearing time. Like every other farm in the district we had our own shearing day at Tynybraich: the Wednesday in the first full week of July. It was important to follow the shearing rota. If we missed our slot because of fog or bad weather we'd have to wait another ten days or even longer, until the district timetable had been completed.

We spent a long time preparing for shearing. The ewes would have their tails and rears cleaned and sheared in May, a practice called *tocio*. This made shearing easier and prevented maggots from infesting them. The ewes were dipped in June, when the farmers dammed the stream, forcing their sheep through the water. Great fun was had at the end of the day when the sheepdogs suffered the same fate.

Then came shearing day itself. Hundreds of sheep were driven into the pens, their desperate bleats filling the air. Up to thirty men sheared in a semi-circle, wielding their shears over sheep lying with their feet trussed together, snipping away all day, cleaving flesh and fleece. The wool seemed to fall away of its own accord. It was the children who put a length of string into the shearer's hand to tie up the next sheep. They were hard to handle unless trussed.

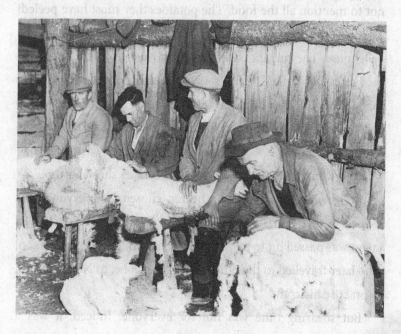

Bob, second from left, shearing

It was the children too who had the privilege of pressing a distinct pitch insignia on the sheep's shoulder. The women wrapped the wool, folding the border of each fleece inwards and rolling it tightly into a soft white ball.

In my mind's eye, I bury my face in the smell of lanolin and feel the softness of the newly shorn wool.

For the women, shearing day was exhausting. They had to make space for thirty men in the kitchen, ensuring there were enough plates, knives, forks, spoons, bowls and cups for everyone, not to mention all the food. The potatoes they must have peeled! The bowlfuls of rice pudding they must have cooked in the bakehouse. The currant cakes they must have griddled. The bread they must have baked. All to satisfy the hunger of men. And how many times did they refill the kettle dangling over the fire, or run to the pantry to fetch milk, to make enough tea to quench the shearers' thirst?

The women were the key to a successful shearing day.

Bob became an excellent shearer, chosen by everyone who wished to take a prized specimen to be exhibited at a show. His talent was passed on to his son, and in due course to his son's son, who later travelled to the other side of the globe, to New Zealand, to practise his craft.

But shearing time was not for everyone. Indeed, it was a detestable time for William, who was confused by the mess of makeshift pens in the farmyard, the barred gates which hindered him. He was bothered by the braying and the endless to-ing and fro-ing of so many people. He'd lose his way and lose his temper.

Of course, the disorder of shearing day was nothing compared to the anarchy of snow. William would lose his way in any layer of white. Unable to feel the free movement of his feet, the echo of his footstep muffled by snow, he often got lost.

Once, on his way towards the farmhouse, he was caught in heavy snow and got lost. There was no sign of him. We searched every field and path all the way to Maesglasau, shouting his name, whistling, called out to him again and again. Our voices echoed throughout the cwm.

Finally, Bob chanced to look towards the mountain, and he was spotted. From the midst of snow-covered bracken a red-gloved hand was seen waving; we knew it belonged to William. We listened and heard his voice. He was calling for help.

It's a mystery how he got there, high on the flanks of our snow-banked mountain.

William never ventured out at night – not for his own protection, but for ours. After all, night and day were one to him. He stayed indoors because he knew that if he got lost in the dark we wouldn't find him. With eyes wide open, we'd be blinder than him.

Indeed, we often took advantage of his "other" sight when we needed to escort the children at night from my parents' new bungalow at the foot of the mountain, back up to the farmhouse.

Rarely did William lose his way during his peregrinations around the farm's pathways. He was an extraordinary figure in his dark, full-length coat and oversized Wellingtons. His head aslant, he listened for the slightest sound. His points of orientation were unchanging: the feel of the ground under his feet; the sound of the running stream; the whisper of hazel leaves in the copse by the lower field; the certainty of the gatepost and the click of the latch as the gate closed.

It took a whole day for him to find his bearings again when he returned to Tynybraich after his occasional outings. It was painful to watch his errors of step, as he walked into posts and trapped himself in corners. He'd rub his eyes with his knuckles. But we were obliged to let him err, for he followed the singular trail of his acute senses. His hearing was a form of sight: he'd strike posts and walls, and trace the echo.

A change in surroundings could cause confusion. Obstacles in his path. We'd bruise his dignity through lack of thought.

It was William's job every Friday afternoon to fetch bread from Tynybraich and take it down to our parents' bungalow. Every week he took three loaves. By habit he put one loaf in a bag which he carried in one hand, with the second loaf in a similar bag in his other hand and the third tucked tightly underneath an arm. Thus he would walk from Tynybraich towards the bungalow. But one particular Friday a bundle of hay was left unwittingly in his pathway. William fell, then rolled downwards, all the way to the bottom of the hill. We rushed to his aid. He continued to lie, supine, in the grass, his shock slowly turning to rage. But the loaves of bread were still held tight in his hands, and the third stayed fast under his arm.

That was a measure of his devotion to the paths and responsibilities of life.

It was in this careful and dutiful way that he completed all his tasks on the farm. It was William, for instance, who turned the handle of the churn at buttermaking. He'd sit there patiently rotating the handle until the butter was made. After churning he'd carry the left-over buttermilk in a pail, along the uneven path to Mother, without spilling a single drop.

Moreover, he had his own work, as copyist and editor of braille texts for the R.N.I.B. Like Lewis his younger brother, William was an excellent linguist who could work in twelve different languages, including Hebrew, Russian and Greek. He'd be at his desk for hours on end, reading and copying; the heavy tip-tapping of his braille machine, together with the tinkle of the bell at the end of each line, a regular and constant sound.

After completing each text he asked us to do the final check before the item was sent to the R.N.I.B. in London. Usually I or Mother undertook this task. Only we had the patience.

We'd sit with William for hours, the braille typescripts spread out. He would read through the text, comparing it against the original. When his soft fingers encountered an error he would instruct us to "delete" or "strengthen" one of the six braille dots as required:

"Delete top left."

"Delete bottom right."

Our task then was to rub out the molehill of a dot with a knitting needle until the paper was smooth again, thus changing and correcting the letter. It was a laborious process. We could be at it for hours "deleting" with a knitting needle.

The finished typescripts were placed in grey boxes and sent to the R.N.I.B. in London. William would intone the address in his rather grand English – "Two Hundred and Twenty Four, Great Portland Street, London" – while one of us filled in the labels as rapidly as we could.

Every time he stuck the labels to the boxes I was amazed at the way he did it. First, he held the label to his lips to find the glued side – the side which stuck to his mouth. Then he'd grasp the label by its upper corners, carefully, and start to lick the glue. For William, even that simple act required care. He'd push his tongue out in a genteel way and proceed to wet the label, moving in an orderly way from left to right. On reaching the end of each swathe he would retract his tongue and then start on the next bit of gum.

And so the very tip of his tongue would shuttle to and fro, from left to right, until the label had been thoroughly licked.

More than once I heard my father murmur that William's fastidiousness was his only handicap. For me, William was one of the great wonders of the cwm.

Every day had to run like clockwork, with breakfast at eight, a cup of tea at ten, lunch at noon, tea at four and supper at seven. If he woke up late he'd be out of sorts for the rest of the day.

Even his meals followed a set pattern. At teatime he'd eat two and a half slices of buttered bread with jam. He'd eat a slice and a half initially, using a spoon to collect any bits of jam on his plate until every morsel was gone. Then he'd quickly drink a cup of tea. After that he'd eat the remaining slice of bread and butter. Then a slice of cake, followed by a second cup of tea, also drunk quickly. And lastly he'd pop a mint imperial in his mouth to end the meal.

He'd shuffle from his own room to the kitchen in a pair of leather slippers. For his meal he'd change into another pair, made of tweedy twill. For his trips outside he'd change into Wellington boots. No matter how many times a day he was obliged to change his footwear, he stuck to this arrangement.

In the same manner, he would think nothing of spending an entire afternoon unpicking knots in a piece of string, untying each entanglement until he held, victoriously, a straight, smooth cord in front of him.

My brother William was a kind man, sociable and sympathetic. In contrast to his three brothers he got no pleasure from debating, and on many occasions I saw him return to his adversary to apologise.

More than anything he loved a chat, and since he'd read widely he had an amazing store of knowledge on many subjects. When I cut his hair his head would move in concurrence with his conversation, which made me nervous with the scissors. He listened avidly to the radio, to the operas of Gilbert and Sullivan, and to his favourite football and cricket commentators. He knew the names of every player in every team.

His radio was his lifelong friend and companion. Indeed, by means of his radio William knew more about the world beyond Cwm Maesglasau than the rest of us put together.

Sometimes this was made evident in unexpected ways. There was an occasion when a petition was circulated in Dinas Mawddwy opposing a proposal to let pubs open their doors on Sundays. It was signed by the vast majority of local residents, and the teetotallers of Tynybraich were no exception. The relevant sheet of paper was taken to William and its message made known to him. But to the astonishment of his abstinent relatives, he refused to sign it. Despite many prompts by his family he held his ground, though alcohol had never passed his lips.

"I don't know what's got into him, I really don't." Mother was shocked.

It was through the medium of radio that William also learned about the latest technological advances. He was the first to tell us, for example, about the video machine which would enable people to tape programmes on the television and watch them a second time. This technology was useless to him, but he expressed a keen interest in it. He also revealed that a new type of oven would use "microwave" technology to heat food (without becoming hot itself). We scorned such ideas, until they came to fruition years later.

William was our chief link with Gruffydd in Herefordshire. He wrote a weekly braille letter to his brother, sending him all the latest news from Tynybraich. He'd type it with great dedication every Thursday morning. Likewise, Gruffydd's weekly letter arrived regularly every Saturday. The brothers began their letters using the same formula every week. William always opened by saying: "Well, here I am again . . ." Gruffydd always with the words, "Very many thanks for Bill's letter . . ."

At the beginning of the thirties Bob married Katie, daughter of a farming family from Tyddyn Rhys y Gader at Aberdyfi. My parents and William moved to a new bungalow, as tradition dictated, to make way for Bob and Katie to set up home in the farmhouse. I stayed at the farmhouse with them: that was my workplace as seamstress.

The birth of their first son in 1936 was a great joy to everyone. Like his grandfather, and his grandfather's grandfather, he, too, was named Evan. I was given the comfort of helping to bring up the first child of the next generation.

William often kept me company in this. He'd sing a lullaby to the baby, and rock the cradle. We were delighted – William more than anyone, perhaps – when we heard a year or so later that a second child was on the way.

Perhaps William was feeling low that day I heard him wondering out loud to Katie about why he'd been put on this Earth: blind, and of no use to anyone. She put her arm around him and reminded him how fond little Evan was of his uncle. Could he not feel the affection in the tight clasp of the little hand around his finger?

Weeks later, at the birth of her second child, Katie died at the hospital in Liverpool. Bob became a young widower with two small children; the elder, Evan, was eighteen months; the younger, Kate, a few hours old.

I will never forget walking into the kitchen at Tynybraich on the dark day that Katie was buried. What I saw in front of me was William, nursing the newborn baby. I recalled the sad question he had posed only weeks before, to a woman who now lay dead. His answer was there: a babe in his arms.

88

The old Tynybraich farmhouse

Though she was approaching her sixtieth year, Mother became a "mother" to Evan and Kate. There was a reversal: my parents moved back to the farmhouse at Tynybraich, and the new bungalow rented to a man called Gruffydd Elis. For the first time, my father had a companion in Maesglasau valley. In those days he was never happier than when wandering the fields with his companion; together they'd take a step forward, pause, then chat. In their mouths a medley of pithy country lore and tobacco plugs, which were then spat out in a tight bullet onto the green grass.

Evan and little Kate were adorable. What a delight it was to watch them playing, as Bob and I had played in the past. Playing bows and arrows in the lower field. Playing house in the roots of the old tree. And playing also on the old cart, with Blodwen the hen still alive in our memories.

Kate delighted in brushing my hair and pretending to paint my nails; Evan's mischief made me laugh into my handkerchief. His indignation at having to attend chapel on Sunday was memorably expressed one morning, as I washed breakfast dishes.

"Why do we have to go to that old chapel again?" he complained to his grandmother.

"Shush, now, Evan bach, that's not the way to talk about chapel."

"Why?"

"It is God's house."

"I've never seen him there."

A heavy sigh from my mother. And then a patient explanation: "We don't *see* the Great Lord, we *feel* him."

"I've never felt him either."

A long pause – Mother had no reply to this. And the little boy's logical mind persisted:

"And anyway, why does he need three houses in Dinas?"

William revelled in the company of children, but when they got under his feet, or left toys underfoot, they provoked his anger. One of their favourite tricks was to put bits of grit on the open pages of his braille book, and then watch his dexterous fingers approaching the extra dots; touching them; pausing; getting confused; re-reading the bogus letter; hesitating, and then realising . . .

"Botheration!"

Despite this mischief they respected their blind uncle and were astonished by his supernatural abilities. Often they'd imitate him at the dinner table, attempting to clear their plates with their eyes shut (though woe betide them if they were spotted).

When it was difficult to settle Evan and Kate at bedtime, it was William who was sent to lie with them. Only he had the patience. He could lie silent and still until they were fast asleep.

Then, gently, William would inch towards the edge of the bed. He'd put his feet on the floor without a sound. Painfully slowly, he'd walk towards the door and place his hand on the latch, turning it gradually. With a sigh of relief, he'd step from the room . . .

"Where are you going, Will?" would come Evan's cry from the dark.

One day we were visited by two men in suits: government employees bringing us gasmasks. There were only two small windows for the eyes. An air-filter covered the nose and mouth. Through those masks we heard nothing but the noise of our own breathing.

It was thus that the Second World War reached Maesglasau valley.

> And for why did they meet in anger, those mighty creatures? The mountains were big enow for them both in our eyes, their sad encounter had no need.
>
> Hugh Jones

Bob joined the Home Guard. William was taken to work at a mechanical factory at Machynlleth. And I put away my sewing machine and went to work on the land, taking on the role of a man.

We received the latest news every evening on the radio, and from friends who lived beyond the defending walls of the cwm. We heard about the evacuees coming from Birmingham. Also about the German Junker 88 aircraft which came down in Montgomeryshire, and whose injured pilot spoke such excellent English that the Welsh-speaking locals who helped him failed to realise he was the enemy. We heard too about the American B17 Flying Fortress which came down for no apparent reason in the hills of Meirionnydd, killing eight of its crew on the Berwyn mountains; another eight were killed on Arenig Fawr. And we heard about the bombing in London, whilst thinking always about our brother, the blind vicar, in its midst.

Gruff was allowed to leave the dangers of England's capital city before the firestorms created by the V1 and V2 bombs in the latter years of the war. But we knew about them, because of what happened to Evelyn King.

A cousin of my grandmother – a woman called Sarah – lived in Pimlico. During the afternoon of July 8, 1944, she was visiting relatives of her husband, Harry King, when the sirens started to wail.

The house she was in was hit directly. They were all killed.

That evening Sarah's daughter, Evelyn, went from work to her aunts' house to accompany her mother home. She rounded the corner and found neither house nor relatives. Smoke rose from the debris, as if from a hellish altar. Black dust rained down.

Evelyn, our orphaned second cousin, came to live with us at Tynybraich, so that she might recover from the shock. She shared a bed with me, suffering nightmares which made her cry out at night. We gave her as much love as we could, but she rarely spoke. Her eyes seemed dead. After the war, Evelyn returned to London to pick up the threads of her lonely life. She never fully recovered from the shock of the blitz.

Many a lowly servant, in summertime, when the day is long and the weather hot, oft yearns in his heart of hearts for the shadows of eventide and the setting of the sun, so that he might rest from his labours.

We met the enemy in flesh and blood in Cwm Maesglasau as in many another valley of rural Wales. In the summer of 1942 an Italian prisoner of war came to us, the first of four visitors from a world we knew nothing of.

Angelo arrived dressed in a uniform which seemed grey against his olive complexion. He stepped from the vehicle and stared at the green valley around him. He gazed with equal surprise at the row of "enemies" awaiting him by the door of the farmhouse: Bob and I as black-haired as he was; Evan and Kate sheltering behind their father's legs.

Bob freed himself from the grasp of his little footmen and

stepped towards the Italian to shake his hand.

"*Bore da.*"

"*Buongiorno.*"

And with that brief interchange, Angelo came into our world.

Soon he was part of everyday life on the farm. He gave thanks every morning for his escape from the calamity of war. And despite suffering prolonged bouts of longing for his wife and children, he gave thanks too for being allowed to spend his internment on a farm. He slept in the small room at the back of the house, and kept a picture of his family, framed in wood, by his bedside. His wife, Susanna, was slim and attractive, with every hair in place; his son and daughter were about the same age as Evan and Kate. He'd call them his "*bambini*", his voice full of emotion.

He worked and ate alongside the family at Tynybraich. Indeed, he and Bob became friends of sorts, as one learned Italian words and the other Welsh ones, communicating happily in the no man's land between languages.

Our own *bambini* learned to count from one to ten in the soft Italian language. And they'd mimic Angelo with his declarations of awe at the cwm's beauty:

"*Che bello!*"

Angelo belonged to a family which kept vineyards in the Frascati region, near Rome. He was amazed by our tradition of temperance. Indeed, he maintained that the steep slopes of Cwm Maesglasau were ideal for growing vines, were it not for the rain.

Living at an angle

On Sundays every Italian prisoner in the district was taken to mass at Newtown. Bob occasionally helped during these excursions. And I believe the rites of the Catholic church filled him with wonder.

After a few months Angelo was forced to leave us. The authorities did not wish the "enemy" to fraternise too much with their hosts.

After Angelo came Piero. He was a rather different creature, with a fiery temper. From his mouth came a stream of religious oaths – *Dio*! and *Maria*! – and when the children were tucked up in bed at night they'd imitate his blasphemous utterances. Piero was an angry man, and who could blame him?

Piero was taken away when, in a fit of temper, he pulled a knife on Father. So the Italian had to go.

Next to arrive was Ernesto. A lanky man, good-natured with not much fighting in his blood. He hailed from Naples and showed the wit of that maritime city. A carpenter by trade, he was hardly seen without a piece of carved wood in his hands. He produced offerings for us every day: wooden spoons for the kitchen, a plate, a large bowl; a wooden boat for Evan, to be sailed in Maesglasau stream; and for Kate, his favourite, an egg cup, simply adorned, and a wooden dolly, which I clothed. Every day was Christmas Day with Ernesto, the carpenter from Naples.

*

On the first of May 1943 another Angelo came among us.

I remember that May Day well. A sunny, cloudless day, with a warm breeze caressing the valley. The leaves of late spring were shining, and the hill above the farmhouse was covered with bluebells.

It was, in my memory at least, a day of freshness and energy, one of those rare days when the whole of creation seems to breathe into the depths of its own being.

I see myself coming out of the house that day. In my arms a bundle of newly washed bedclothes. The door behind me is open.

I raise my eyes. In front of me, at my brother's side, there is a man in prisoner's clothing.

He turns to look. I return his gaze. But I see nothing. All I do is feel. I sense a tremor running through me. Sapping me. Taking my breath away.

I notice Bob staring. I return to my work and walk away. But the land beneath my feet, between the front and the back of Tynybraich farmhouse, seems to sway with every step.

I peg the white linen onto the line, watching it move in May's tender breeze. Then I steady myself and return to my work, as befits a woman approaching forty.

I bow into the machine and work away. The handle on the Singer's wheel keeps slipping; I undo the seams and sew again.

Later, I join my family at the table to welcome the guest.

We enjoyed four months in Angelo's company. Four months of joy, a sort of happiness I had never experienced before. Everything shone in the glow of my feelings; the pewter plates on the dresser, the brass fender, even the farm's rusty implements.

They were four months of learning, also. Learning about someone I could laugh with, be solemn and joyous with, in a natural way. Learning also to hide my feelings; to modulate emotion and subdue the body. I learned how to live a lie; keeping a flood of emotions behind a dam of pride, hesitation and anxiety.

And I learned Italian, though the words were often so close to those of my own language:

"*Ponte*," said Angelo.

"*Pont*," I answered.

Finestra.

Ffenest.

Corona.

Coron.

Corpo.

Corff.

Credere.

Credu.

Celare.

Celu.

In naming the world again, it came into existence anew. And this rebirth happened in the summer of 1943.

Only to die again, when Mussolini was overthrown and Italy's new government yielded to the Allies. The time came to release our prisoners. Angelo was summoned away.

Yes, the end of summer was death itself that year. Each day slipped away. The nights were sleepless, full of memories, full of tears. I could tell no-one.

On the day before he left, Angelo asked to visit the waterfall at the end of Cwm Maesglasau. I went with him.

I do not remember that journey to Maesglasau, walking past the field at Cae Dolau, through Llidiart y Dŵr, the sheep turning to us, the birds falling silent, the river slowing down. All I remember is my hand in his, walking to the end of the world.

And then we reached the light-filled end of the valley. The old ruin stood in silence. The stream glittered in a cascade, a jumble of stones formed a path across the flow. We went upwards, through reeds and nettles, higher and higher up the ravine, quickening our step, losing our breath, to arrive, at last, at the foamy base of the waterfall.

I can see us still, in my mind's eye, as we hesitated before he pulled me under the powerful flow, Maesglasau's quicksilver water shattering around us.

I shall never forget the three hundred yards back towards my home. Clothes soaking wet. Late evening sunshine bathing the world in gold. Each second priceless. Each step painful.

As we approach Tynybraich farmhouse I stop and look at him. And I see the understanding between us which is so easy to feel, so hard to understand.

We return to Tynybraich separately.

I see Angelo saying his farewells, shaking hands with my parents, William and Bob, hugging the children. Hugging me, in the same way.

I see him turn. I see his back. I see the thickness of his hair, his familiar gait.

I did not see him depart. I fainted on the doorstep of Tynybraich. Bob and my father carried me to bed.

> Behold, the days have grown shorter and the sun doth rise
> with no purpose; he hoves into view through the dark and
> foggy air, giving Earth the merest glance with his weak and
> pallid rays; for he stays but a short time, and shies away
> soon enough, as if no joy could be had in viewing the world.
>
> Hugh Jones

I yielded to something that September. I fell into a fever, and was ill for weeks. And when the fever went, it left in its wake a debilitation. I could neither read nor sew nor write a single word.

Everyone was concerned. But no-one – not even my mother – knew the cause.

How could I explain? I could not explain it to myself. The pride. The hesitancy. The fear. And how could one explain the truth of a feeling, when that feeling never really got to exist?

Bob married for a second time in March 1944. His new wife had come to Dinas Mawddwy from Cwm Nant yr Eira – the valley of snow – to stay with her cousin, Mairwen. Her name was Olwen.

As the years passed by she became a dear sister to me and a second daughter to my mother. Another Olwen.

It wasn't easy for Olwen to arrive as a young wife at Tynybraich, and to step into the role of stepmother to Evan and Kate. Yet, she achieved it all with ease. She was that kind of woman. She adapted without fuss to the ways of the family, and we all warmed to her sunny, quiet ways.

My parents and William moved back to the bungalow.

Great joy was felt at the birth of Olwen and Bob's first child in February 1946.

Kate, the little sister, was allowed to choose the name: Mair.

A brother to Mair, called Wyn, was born the following year.

It was the coming of Olwen – her part in shouldering so many household duties – which enabled me to come to a decision regarding my own life. I asked my parents and Bob for permission to go and live in my grandmother's old home at Maesglasau Bach.

The time had come for me to have my own home. I was over forty years old.

Everyone stared in disbelief.

Why live in that remote spot at the end of the valley, keeping company with old ghosts?

I insisted, and the men gave way. They knew me well enough: there would be no turning.

By the spring of 1948 the old house had been made homely. My few possessions were moved by cart from Tynybraich to the far end of Maesglasau valley: a bed, a table, two chairs and a book case; a small gas stove; the Singer sewing machine; my clothes, books, pen and paper, all in a small chest.

There was neither electricity nor running water at Maesglasau Bach. But I had a roof over my head, four walls around me, and a door which could be shut on the world. There was silence. A defined space for me alone.

I had light from the sun by day and from a candle by night. I had water, always, from Maesglasau stream, in which I could both quench my thirst and cleanse my body.

In the old days, before the coming of the lowland roads, people used these highland tracks in their daily lives. The upland causeways were the country's backbone. It was easier to cross the heights than to ascend and descend the hills of Mid-Wales, and they were safer than the lowlands' treacherous roads. "Our ancestors were people of the heights," writes the historian R. T. Jenkins, "they were people who lived 'on high'. And it can be said of the old Welshman that he was someone who walked from one summit to the next."

I've heard it said that the monks of the middle ages used these trackways as they moved between the abbeys at Strata Florida and Cymer; that Cwm Glan Mynach and Cae'r Abaty above Bwlch y Siglen both got their names from these mendicant monks. And what church, I wonder, gave its name to Cwm yr Eglwys? There's an old tradition, which contradicts academic opinion, that the "clas" which forms the second part of the name "Maesglasau" was a hostel for monks. It must have been this story that inspired a Victorian rhymester to compose the following poem on the empty page of one of our family's old books:

In Dinas Mawddwy parish stands a monastery alone,
Where once upon a time a burdened monk did moan.

A far off lonely spot, loved by holy wight,
Wondrous romantic, below a fountain white.

Now the monastery rooms and walls lie starkly bare,
Though bearing witness to a former grandeur rare.

*My ancestors, too, walked "from one summit to the next", taking the
high road when they went to harvest the peat with their cutting
irons, dragging their peat sledges behind them, piled high with black
bricks – the rotted remains of ancient forests, now our winter fuel.
They walked these high pathways too when they went to worship
every Sabbath, walking all the way from Cwm Maesglasau to the
old church at Mallwyd.*

*It was a poet, not a road-builder, who changed all that. Almost
two centuries ago Hugh Jones, the hymnist and translator who was
born and brought up at Maesglasau, returned from London to his
native home, fired by Calvinism. Swayed by his words, the families
of Tynybraich and Maesglasau became nonconformists. Their path
towards faith took a different direction: the hike over the hills
to Mallwyd church was abandoned; in its stead came the walk along
a lowland lane to chapel at Dinas Mawddwy.*

The hymns of Hugh Jones continue to ring out from that chapel, though weaker year by year. But the pilgrims' pathways of old have disappeared. "As Man's highland existence fell away," wrote the historian, "so did his pathways fall with him."

There is no doubt that the uplands were once busier than they are today. Indeed, this high plateau on the border between Merioneth and Montgomery was frequented by the Red Bandits of Dugoed. Five centuries ago these outlaws tracked and robbed their victims without mercy. A cluster of billhooks was lodged in the chimney at Maesglasau to prevent their sudden attack, and remains there to this day. But the Red Bandits' caves remain hidden in the hills; their ghosts come alive in the low mists, and the wailing of women and orphaned children haunts the bitter wind of the Oerddrws Pass. And when sunset fires the moorland on a summer's evening the memory of spilt blood seems to colour the land itself.

I stand and listen. Nothing is heard except the bleat of a sheep, the croak of a crow, or the harpistry of a lark as it flits from the heather under my foot. The lark rises, borne higher and higher by the fluency of its own wings, and I follow its flight. I see the forked-tailed silhouette of a kite, hovering. Beyond the kite, the wing-shadows of two peregrine falcons in dance. It is pairing time: the smaller male feigns an attack on the female. Soon we shall see the falcon's mottled eggs on the cliff-face at Maesglasau, away from other nests and human habitation.

Falco peregrinus: *the most rapid of all pilgrims, reaching its end with a missile's speed and precision. Detested by gamekeepers and egg thieves, it lived on the edge of extinction. Today it is still rare, in these parts at least. A sublime bird, dark of cheek, blue-grey of body and wings, its belly a speckled white. Its clear, repetitive cry is electrifying.*

Only once did I see it hunt. That sky-chase is imprinted on my memory. It was in Cwm yr Eglwys one morning. A falcon hovered high in the air.

Suddenly a grouse flew out of the forest into open ground. I stood and watched the drama unfold. There was no hope for the grouse. Paralysed with fear and awe I watched as the falcon swept back its wings and plummeted at whistling speed; two hundred miles per hour, they say.

Then came the strike. An explosion of brown feathers. The grouse's backbone snapped in two. A single strike finished it.

It's a merciful death, they say, that of the prey of the peregrine falcon. But for me, an old woman in her nineties, staring death in the face and willing my own continuance, no death is merciful.

Yet, I know that on that day I rejoiced in the clean kill of a steel bullet sheathed in feathers.

4

He fashions a chariot from the clouds and flies on the wings of the wind.

Hugh Jones

What is family? An anchor which holds us in place. It holds us secure in a storm. It holds us back in fair weather. It is a blessing and a burden – for the young, especially, and for those who seek freedom.

One of life's astonishing moments is when we realise that we have suddenly become that anchor. This sudden shift is shocking and instantaneous. It is the shift of generations. We are flung without warning into the air, then plummet the depths of salt water. Then the anchor takes hold. Everything settles.

For some people, this happens at the birth of the first child, when they learn the skill of holding someone tight without holding them back.

For me, it was the death of my father which propelled me

from one generation to the next. Strange, for I was then already a woman approaching fifty years of age, strands of silver multiplying in my dark hair. But until then I had been a girl. Father's girl. And he was the head of the family. It had nothing to do with age.

None of us was ever "close" to Father. For him I was a woman, a younger version of Mother, helping her to fulfil the duties of a farmer's wife. Preparing food. Cups of tea. Submitting. Comforting.

For years I suffered in silence. This detestable tradition of woman as maidservant! But as I grew older, acceptance became easier. Father weakened as he grew old. His need for the anchor of home grew more apparent. I came to understand him; learned not to fear his judgement. I finally saw how dependent he was.

What I see now is a man who needed some rest after a hard day's labour. He did not have the time to succour his children. He would leave the house in the small hours to complete his work on the mountain, taking his lunch with him, parcelled in his pocket. He'd be away all day. Only in the setting sun would we see him again. He needed tea, supper, his pipe and silence on the hearth. There wasn't the time to indulge in fatherhood.

Bob had most to do with him, of course. But they were so different. Father was a conversationalist; Bob a reasoner and debater. Father loved the pithy remark, Bob the paragraph. Father loved farming, Bob hated it. My father was a countryman, Bob a politician.

Gruffydd, William and Lewis had had little chance to get to know their father. Estranged from the beginning by a physical chasm, the distance between them widened with the boys' "gentlemanly" education at Worcester College. And Father wasn't the type to seek a compromising route between two different natures. To reach him, you had to do the walking: up and down every hill and dale. He was there to be accepted.

I believe now that his distance from us was part shyness, part impatience. This was the temperament that prompted him, each time we had English visitors, to take to his bed mid-afternoon, or to send away their children with the macaronic command: "Go *ffordd acw*! Away!"

It was Mother who translated Father's needs and wishes, even to us, his own children. It was she who read and interpreted him. Her task was to explain his moods, his brusque answers and outward indifference. She was the mediator. She told us of his exhaustion after work; his right to peace. It was Mother who told Gruffydd, William and Lewis about their father, explaining what was important to him, so that they might understand. It was she who stressed his strengths. His kindness. His stubborn loyalty. His care. His love. With tears in her eyes, she would remind us of his pain when the boys went to school; his bitterness when our unbaptised baby sister, Olwen Mai, could not be buried until the sun had set. She made sure we remembered how he'd cared for

Ieuan in his illness, chewing bits of meat into digestible morsels for "the little boy", placing them in his mouth in the hope that meat would give him strength.

I think of these accounts, and hear – somewhere in my head – always my mother's voice. Her grace and natural intelligence impressed me then. It astounds me now.

I spent countless evenings with my parents around the big chimney at Tynybraich, and in later years at the fireside in their new bungalow. There would be no sound except the occasional rustle as the fire settled in the grate; the ticking of the carriage clock; Mother's knitting needles clicking. Father would stare into the flames or snooze. He never read. I would work on a patchwork quilt or repair some item of clothing, before getting up and taking my leave, walking home in darkness to the end of the cwm.

During those evenings I never dared to start a conversation with Father. My role was to be by his side and to say nothing. He was my father. I was his daughter. That was the end of it.

Yet, during those long silent hours together by the hearth our quiet relationship developed into fullness. The silence we shared grew as a bond between us: white and warm, like pure linen. And when Father died that fabric went with him, as a shroud; in its place came a colder silence.

Thus, in 1950, a stitch was unpicked in the fabric of my own existence.

But Evan Jones of Tynybraich did not die alone. As one of those who paid tribute to him said, a whole way of life went with him. A way of life which allowed a man to keep a vial of strychnine and a set of false teeth in the same waistcoat pocket. He'd been a true "character" of rural life and a wonderful talker. Was it not said that a fence had to be raised between him and his fellows on shearing day, for his ceaseless talk slowed the shearers' work?

I remember smiling on hearing this tribute to the man of field and farmyard. This great talker was a man of silence when he came indoors. And for me, his death was that of a father, not of a type.

Bob became head of the family. I became sister to the head. And I heard the rattle of a chain as it unwound, the silence as the chain fell, the strike of the anchor against land.

This was the shift of generations.

The children came to us more often, no longer in fear of their grandfather's dark moods. Evan and Kate were "big children" now, going to Dolgellau on their own, soon to finish school. It was Mair and Wyn who kept us company, entertaining me and Mother.

There wasn't a minute's peace and we were interrogated daily by the two dark-headed children whose favourite words were *how* and *why* – followed by *who, when* and *where*. They amazed us with the responses to their own questions, though Mother was often shocked by their unorthodox minds.

Why are there clouds in the sky?
Because God has been shearing the angels.

Why are the clouds moving?
So that God can get to Dolgellau.

Why is the sky blue?
So we can see the clouds.

Why is the sun yellow?
Because God churned the moon.

Why do all women knit?
Because they can't shear.

Why is night dark?
So that we can be like William.

Why does the wind blow?
To keep itself warm.

Why is it raining?
Because God's river is leaking.

> Why do waterfalls drop down?
> *Because it's lonely at the top of Maesglasau.*

> Why are William and Lewis and Uncle Gruff blind?
> *Because they can see better in the dark.*

They played passionately: hide and seek in the cowshed or around the pigsty and hen hut; playing "house" in the roots of the oak tree; playing school, which delighted Mair; playing bows-and-arrows until the makeshift arrows went astray.

They'd rush headlong towards us, blaming each other, recounting their adventures, quenching their thirst with water from the well at the back of the bungalow. There was a year between them, just like me and Bob. I loved their daily exploits. It was a reminder of our own play decades earlier. Mair would command. Wyn would obey . . . momentarily – until he got tired of his role as pupil to the teacher, patient to the nurse, baby to the mother – and ran away to seek his father at work, tracing him by the barking of dogs. In tears, Mair would come to her aunt for comfort and a Rich Tea biscuit, moistened in a cup of tea. Wyn was too young for tea.

I delighted in their company, my middle-aged flesh soothed by the touch of their hands. I wondered how it might have felt to have children of my own. To this day I thank the generosity of their mother Olwen, who never once showed any possessiveness. She allowed me many memorable hours with her growing children.

Both children were intrigued by my sewing machine. How amazing, to create a pencil case, a tool bag, a teddy, a rag doll, merely by linking a few rags and turning a wheel. For Mair and Wyn the Singer was a magical instrument, its needle a golden wand. They'd stare in wonder at my fingers daring to approach the needle. And once, as I pricked my finger, they stared in dismay at the sight of red blood flowing from the flesh of adults.

This awe of technology was nothing new. My mother had a story about a godly old man who had seen the first steam train in mid-Wales. As it disappeared into a tunnel the man exclaimed that God himself had swallowed the infernal chariot. Similarly awed, my great-uncle, the poet J. J. Tynybraich, had written a strict-metre poem about "Steam". Composed at the peak of Victorian industrial optimism, the poet saw the technology of steam as a magical substance that demanded respect and fear:

Is it an angry fiend – escaped
From the fearful furnace of destruction?
No! It's the impish spirit of fluidity,
The soul of water on its way.

Terrible power! But it must be bound – before
It does any work for you.
Freedom will destroy it –
In frightful bondage lies its power.

Steam makes the wide world – a place
To play tricks with space;
For steam, it's just a jaunt
Across the Globe's wet face.

How amazing is science,
What feats it attains!
As it powers ever onwards
With its mighty gains.

What will it do – what will it not!
Seeing is believing, witness we must!

I wonder what J. J. would have said about the technologies that
came to play an increasingly important part in our farming life
after the Second World War. His delight in modern science
suggests that the old bard would have appreciated the coming of
our water turbine, for example. This was built by Bob and Evan to
generate electricity for Tynybraich, and they, in turn, were advised

by a man called Roland Evans, a self-taught electrician and owner of the Turnpike Garage at Dinas Mawddwy.

At the bottom of the hill, where the road to the farm crossed Maesglasau stream, a shed was built, and in it Bob, Evan and Roland Evans assembled the machine which could turn water into light.

Some time later we were all called down to the shed to witness the "miracle" of hydroelectric power. It was an amazing sight, as the flow of the stream moved the turbine. Unceremoniously the equipment was switched on. We held our breath. Very slowly a faint yellow light glowed in the bulb at the end of a cable. Slowly strengthening, within a few seconds it shone brightly.

I stared, dazzled, words failing me. This was the birth of a new age, here, in a lowly shed on the narrow bank of Maesglasau stream.

Thus, the waters of Maesglasau, you might say, brought light to the world. In yet another way, the stream gave of her own energies to help us. It is the stream – and the trusty turbine – which provides electricity for Tynybraich to this day.

After the turbine came two other devices to lighten our workload in the house: an electric oven and a washing machine. The first was useful; its heat was clean and constant. The second was nothing less than an emancipation – a maid to a maid. It did away with the crushing labour of the weekly wash; the red raw

Bob and Evan and the water turbine

knuckles caused by rubbing and scrubbing, and calluses caused by mangling; the hard, rough hands of soda soap and hot water. All we had to do now was put the clothes into the machine and keep an eye on it while doing the rest of the housework. It was no longer necessary to allocate the whole of Monday to do the dreaded washing.

On Wednesday mornings I would take the washing from the bungalow up to Tynybraich farmhouse, looking forward to a cup of tea with Olwen. A half-hour of leisure. Chatting and laughing. Exchanging recipes and patterns. Discussing the weather or the produce at the show. Talking of the children's progress. These half hours were free time in which we could be sisters.

Towards the beginning of the 1950s, if I remember correctly, Cwm Maesglasau heard the sound of its first telephone, a new apparatus which allowed Lewis and Gruffydd to phone home once a week. We'd be there without fail to answer their calls. I think the ring of the telephone meant as much as the voice of an angel to my mother during her last few years.

Television came late to Tynybraich. Radio waves could not reach the far end of the cwm, and a new receiver was raised on the side of Cwm yr Eglwys – and raised again and again after every storm.

As a matter of fact, Tynybraich went to television, rather than vice versa. In 1964 the journalist John Roberts Williams came to interview us for the BBC's *Heddiw* news programme. He'd heard an amazing story about the "three blind brothers" from Tynybraich and wanted to make a short film.

The cameras came to record the journeys of my three brothers, away from Cwm Maesglasau into the world. Starting with their education at Worcester their stories were followed up to the present, with Gruffydd an Anglican minister at Little Marcle in Herefordshire; Lewis working as a telephonist with the Ministry of Labour at Nottingham, and William acting as a braille copyist and multilingual editor at Tynybraich.

We went to see the film's showing at a friend's house in Dinas Mawddwy.

It opens with a panoramic shot of Tynybraich farmhouse, nestling in a fold of land like an infant in a mother's arm. The title of the programme is stamped in white letters over this scene – "*O! Tyn y Gorchudd*", "Oh, pull aside the veil" – the opening line of the hymn by Hugh Jones of Maesglasau. In the background the Mawddwy male voice choir is heard singing T. Llew Jones' strict-metre poem to Cwm Maesglasau.

Then comes the narrator, Aled Rhys William's voice declaring that Tynybraich had once been home to the famous Harpist of Mawddwy. He recounts an anecdote about my grandfather, Robert Jones, "who turned the cart over because he was reading his Bible instead of looking where he was going". There are camera shots of our stream flowing between bracken and rushes, a sheepdog running hither and thither, black cattle grazing, then raising their heads to look inquisitively into the camera. We see Wyn raking the hay, a cockerel crowing on a gate, and Bob and Evan in a sheep-fold, grasping the animals and sending them splashing through the dip. William is pictured with a bucket in his hand, walking uphill from the bungalow to fetch buttermilk. His head is aslant, as if he could sense the eye of the camera.

The narrator recites the history of the three blind brothers. There is a picture of Gruff in his clerical collar on the lawn of his

Georgian rectory in Herefordshire. In his formal Welsh, Gruff tells the story of his ordination at Southwark in London. With his dry humour he recounts further anecdotes: his first baptism when he held the child upside-down; that time he bathed his infant daughter in total darkness – and the little girl did not say a word. He is seen with his wife Christine and the three children, Elizabeth, Richard and Hugh. He is seen walking with his white stick to the ancient church at Little Marcle – a thousand years old – "almost exactly the same age as Tynybraich." He is shown reading from his braille Bible, pronouncing the words in his formal English accent, his supple fingers gliding over the pages: *Here endeth the first lesson.*

Lewis is next, filmed at his work at a telephone exchange in Nottingham. He mentions the fact that he had some sight as a child; how grateful he is for having seen the colour of bluebells, the wild rose in the hedge, the sun in the sky. He talks about his work with the Samaritans, and how he'd helped a man on the brink of suicide by asking him what he'd like Lewis to see, should he ever regain his sight. Slowly, as he described a particular scene, hope came to the man's voice. Finally, Lewis is pictured with his wife Rachel, together with their three children, Isobel, Bronwen and Dominic. And the camera follows him as he walks towards a telephone box in Nottingham.

A phone rings in the kitchen at Tynybraich. William answers.

And now his tale is told. He is shown at work, editing braille texts in a dozen languages, including works such as the *Hebrew-English Lexicon*. Mother is seen knitting socks in her chair by the dresser, the willow pattern plates in rows behind her. Then Mother and William are seen working together in complete harmony on a braille version of the novel, *O Law i Law*, by T. Rowland Hughes. Mother reads the original; William compares, then copies.

This film, so full of familiar images, was also a revelation. We had never before seen the daily lives of Gruff and Lewis in England, so far from Cwm Maesglasau.

It was so sad when the film ended, as if a dream had ended abruptly. It lasted a mere fifteen minutes, though filming had gone on for days.

William sat between myself and Mother throughout, holding our hands. I remember looking at him afterwards. He had contributed to something – a visual representation of himself – which he could not partake of. His life had been celebrated in a medium which was, in the context of his own existence, largely meaningless.

It was a bittersweet experience for me, then, a quarter of a century later, when I received a videotape copy of the programme from the B.B.C. Archives. Wyn had the necessary equipment to play the film, and we all met in the parlour at Tynybraich to watch the "old fashioned" black-and-white film. It was with terrible longing, mingled with a painful joy, that I saw Mother resurrected on the small screen; Gruff alive too, and William. Our old life came flooding back. There were moments when I felt myself drowning.

I did not weep much. I stubbornly kept the tears in, not wanting to detract from my family's enjoyment.

But when I returned to the privacy of my home, knowing that the babble of the stream would drown my own sound, I could barely shut the door before the tears came. I wept as I had never wept before. I wept through the night – until my bony body weakened.

The greatest pain was the lie perpetrated by the film. It seemed to say that nothing changed, yet showed clearly that nothing lasted. It "immortalised" the visible world. Yet, I – who had been invisible in the film – was the only one who still lived. And more than anything, I resented the way my own multi-coloured memories had been obscured by searing images in black and white.

Back in the 1960s, when that short film was broadcast, and when the miracle of television was still new, it created quite a stir. Gruff, William and Lewis became local celebrities. I agreed with the general opinion that Bob, the eldest of the four brothers, should have received more attention. After all, it was the blindness of his three brothers which had decreed his fate, obliging him to stay on the farm.

He had dreamt of a life as a doctor. And it was true that he had saved his own life and that of others many times by knowing how to treat a life-threatening wound. There were many miles between Tynybraich and the nearest hospital. There was that time he fell while rescuing a sheep on the rocks above Maesglasau. He tore a large vein in his wrist and the blood poured from this wound. He was alone in a remote place. But Bob stemmed the flow of blood by tying a length of baling twine around the top of his arm. He struggled down to the valley floor and dragged himself to the farmhouse, and was only then rushed to hospital.

Bob was an unwilling farmer. He was most happy reading and reasoning. His great love was history books, political biographies and the memoirs of great men. He had no time for literature, and retained a Calvinist distrust of the novels I read.

He learned to escape from the confines of the hill farmer's life by becoming a county councillor and a magistrate. He was an uncompromising Labourite, and was dismayed – to say the least – by his wife's instinctive support for Plaid Cymru. I remember accompanying Olwen in the car at election times, and the minute Tynybraich had gone out of view Olwen would stop the car – with mischief in her eyes – and place a large Plaid Cymru banner on the side window of the car. She'd drive over the Oerddrws Pass to Dolgellau, park it on the Marian where everyone could see it, then drive back over the Pass at the end of the afternoon, still waving the nationalist flag. The moment we passed Ffridd, almost within sight of Tynybraich, Olwen would stop the car and remove the banner, carefully folding it and putting it away in the glove compartment, ready for next Friday's trip to Dolgellau. Bob was never the wiser about the political duplicity of his Morris Marina.

I myself felt quietly envious of their daughter, Mair, who was by now a student at Bangor University, because she lived amid the excitement of the 1960s Welsh-language protests, rather than following a nunnish life in a remote cwm like I did.

As a result of his work with the National Farmers' Union in Merioneth, Bob got to see the world beyond Maesglasau, going to meetings in London, and later Brussels. He loved travelling, returning with many stories. One of his favourites concerned a visit he made to London with one of his acquaintances, a man who had never travelled far from Dinas Mawddwy. Arriving in Trafalgar Square, this man was amazed by the tumult of people and cars. Thinking of the Annual Fair at Dolgellau, or the August Show at Dinas, he walked up to a nearby policeman and asked: "What's going on here today, then?"

Only once did I accompany Bob and Olwen to London. I was amazed: the unbroken traffic, the huge buildings, the Babel of peoples. What astonished me most was the noise, deafening, muddling me. I closed my ears to it and did not open them again until I got home.

Soon after the film about "the three blind brothers" was broadcast, Mother's mind began to cloud over. That was to be expected, perhaps, in a woman over eighty years old. Yet, it made me uneasy. On the day she broke the rule of a lifetime by reaching for her knitting on a Sabbath, I knew something was wrong. Olwen also noticed.

Mother began to show signs of increasing confusion. Uncharacteristically, she'd give a prickly response to a question. She'd contradict. Pretend she couldn't hear. She often disappeared into her own world. This from a woman known for her gentleness and care.

She declined rapidly. Before long it was clear to us that she suffered from that terrible disease, Alzheimer's. She was moved from the bungalow back to the farmhouse at Tynybraich to be cared for.

It was nightmarish to hear her call in the small hours, thinking it was time to get up. Wyn, who slept in the bedroom next door to her, would go to her and ease her back towards sleep.

Mother's illness was more troubling for William than anyone. Since the death of my father, the needs of "Wil Bach" – "Little Will" – had been at the centre of Mother's life. She provided for him, did everything she could to smooth his way. He in turn came to depend on her, as the rest of us depended on the clock.

Now – aged over fifty – he had to cope without her.

William bridged that gap between his healthy mother and his sick mother through physical contact. Each morning he went to her and lay on the bed by her side. This always calmed her. When she was ready, William helped her to rise, dress, come downstairs and enter the kitchen. This daily ritual became a genuine comfort to them both.

Under Olwen's careful guidance William gradually learned to manage on his own. He learned how to pour tea into his cup, by placing his finger on the rim to gauge the level. He got into the habit of taking his supper with him from the farmhouse to the bungalow, preparing it himself when he got there. After tea each afternoon he put on a coat and his Wellingtons. Methodically, he scanned his basket with his hand to check the constituents of his supper: a Tupperware box with a slice of meat or hard-boiled eggs, bread and butter wrapped in greaseproof paper, a slice of currant loaf, a flask of tea, some milk in a brown medicine bottle. All in place. Then he'd begin his slow journey across the farmyard and down the hill towards his own home.

I went to Mother each afternoon, leaving the far end of the cwm to be with her. She looked as sweet as ever: clear eyes, snow-white hair and fair complexion.

But she was not the same woman. She had been transformed by her illness. She recognised neither me nor Bob. She was obstinate. She'd sulk. She vanished before our eyes into another world. We could not reclaim her. She was a creature of our own flesh, sustained by the same breath of life. Mother and I had always been particularly close. But now she was a stranger. Even as I embraced her, she went further and further away. The disease stole her. My only hope is that she never knew the cruel distortion of her own self.

The illness lasted four years, worsening pitilessly. Mother died in her bed at Tynybraich on December 20, 1968. We had lost her long before.

I shall never forget her radiant, peaceful face against the white sheet, her still body, which had laboured through her long life. Another stitch unravelled. My hold on the world loosened again.

There is an essay written in commemoration of my father's father. The words are truly fitting for Mother too:

> That self-effacing will . . . was the mysterious component
> of his strength and greatness. His rich inner life had been
> hidden from view. And he himself was unaware of that
> which struck all who saw him – that the skin on his face
> shone brightly.

Decades later, my longing for Mother still takes my breath away.

I spent Christmas 1968, like every other Christmas, at Tynybraich. This was a dark Christmas. I barely remember it. The only star that shone was a visit from Bob's grandchildren on Boxing Day. Evan came to see us with his wife, Mair, and their three children, Gareth, Ann and Eleri. And Kate came from Shrewsbury with her husband Wyn, her son Geraint and a baby – Alwyn – on the way.

I had meant to return to my own home on New Year's Day, but snowstorms and snowdrifts on the path prevented me. I departed at last on the Feast of Epiphany – January 6, 1969. The stream at Maesglasau had frozen hard.

> The tips of the trees wear white lace and the eaves hold
> sharp swords. Everything endeavours to hide its head
> under whatever guard it can find, to save itself from the
> tempests and icy frost which seek to obliterate it.
>
> Hugh Jones

I remember shutting my door on the cold cwm and promising myself I'd go travelling.

But who in mid-Wales in the 1960s had heard of an "old maid" going travelling alone? There was no hope. I did not have the means. I had no car, could not pay for bus, train or ship – let alone the price of an aeroplane ticket.

All I had was a lift to Dolgellau every Friday afternoon in Olwen's Morris Marina. But in Dolgellau there was a library, and it was there that I started to travel through books – and my imagination.

I pored over a world atlas by the light of a paraffin lamp. But I knew already where I'd go. I had a long-standing wish to visit Europe's great cities.

Through picture books and travelogues, I started from the kitchen of my home, leaving by ship and destined for France. I spent three days in Paris, where I travelled on the bateau mouche along the Seine, awestruck by the magnificent buildings on its banks. I gaped at the treasures of the Louvre. I took trains to the beautiful cities of Belgium and Holland: Ghent, Leuven, Antwerp, Amsterdam. Onwards to Scandinavia, to Copenhagen, Oslo, Stockholm and Helsinki, coming back via the wonderful cities of Germany: Berlin, Cologne and its great cathedral; Munich and its galleries; the damaged glories of Dresden and Leipzig. I crossed Charles Bridge in Prague, and followed the footsteps of Kafka. And in Vienna I had the best seat at the opera house, drank coffee with the ghosts of poets and musicians and waltzed at Schönbrunn. Then I travelled on the Danube to Budapest.

I kept my own imaginary travelogue: my impressions, the names of places and people, dates and contacts which did not really exist.

Who would have thought that the whole world could be seen from Maesglasau?

Two cities delighted me more than all others. I went to Istanbul on the Orient Express and stayed at the Pera Palas Hotel. I saw the Golden Horn and the river Bosphorus. Asia lay to the east; Europe to the west. I saw minarets and the domed roofs of mosques. I heard the call of the *muezzin* and gazed at the great Byzantine church of Aghia Sofia, the beauty of the Blue Mosque, the opulence of Topkapi palace, with the Sea of Marmara on one hand, the Black Sea on the other. I saw the Sultan's harem and learned of his concubines. I crossed bridges between rows of fishermen, and saw the graceful devotional dance of the Whirling Dervishes.

But it was in Rome that I lingered longest. I saw the cruel Coliseum and the beautiful square on the Capitoline Hill. I threw pennies into baroque fountains, and walked to the Vatican, submitting to the cold embrace of St Peter's colonnades and placing my hand on St Peter's foot. I would see the Popes' tombs, before rushing back to daylight.

And through all my days in the eternal city I searched for one familiar face, but found his likeness only in sculptures, portraits, in the reflections of fountains, or in echoes of young men's voices.

I cannot remember how long I spent travelling. Whether it was days, weeks, months, I cannot say. It was a time of sweet enthralment, and for the first time in my life I felt carefree. I was away for so long I forgot about home.

As it approached its four hundredth birthday the old house at Tynybraich was demolished. The wind had been whistling through gaps in the windows. The walls had begun to decay. The old hallway had been saturated with damp and cold. Repairing such an old house was too expensive. The money just wasn't there.

And so when I returned from my travels – and woke as if from a dream – I found a new Tynybraich raised on the site of the old. It became a comfortable home for Wyn and his wife – another Olwen. A smaller house was built to accommodate Bob and his own Olwen, both of them grandparents to Aled and Catrin who lived on the farm, and the children of Mair and her husband Emyr – Irfon, Iolo and Angharad.

The years passed. Bob was semi-retired by now and Wyn became head of the household at Tynybraich. Gruff and Lewis became grandfathers, to Gwilym, Lynne and Mark, and Mark himself shared the blindness of his grandfather.

But Gruff died in 1982. He was buried in the graveyard at Little Marcle. I didn't go to his funeral. I no longer wanted to leave the cwm. The stitches that held me there were unravelling too quickly.

A year later, in July 1983, Bob died of lung cancer. His hair had still been black, with just a few streaks of silver. On the day of his funeral Ebenezer Chapel at Dinas Mawddwy overflowed with mourners. The singing was passionate.

Olwen had lost her husband, and Evan, Kate, Mair and Wyn had lost their father. I in turn had lost my brother – my friend for nearly eighty years.

I lost a third brother, William, in 1990. His last few years were cruel. He lost his hearing, as Gruff and Bob had done. He could no longer conduct a conversation with ease. He couldn't hear his beloved radio. His links with the world and with his kin were broken. Walking was hard because of pains in his leg. Of his five senses, only two remained. Touch and taste. He would hold the hand of one of Bob's grandchildren, and a tear would run down his cheek. He would savour his meals, and in tasting each morsel he retained a degree of independence: he could commune with each slice of meat, the bread and butter, the fruit loaf, and the tea that he poured with such dexterity into his own cup.

With Lewis I continued to speak regularly on the phone. We talked about books, occasionally reminiscing and often laughing. But my closest companion in the last decade of the twentieth century was Olwen, my sister-in-law.

We had differing personalities. Olwen was amiable and even-tempered, always ready to forgive and forget. I, like the rest of the Tynybraich clan, was apt to be stubborn and obdurate, often moody or lost in thought.

Yet, Olwen and I had been friends from the moment she'd arrived at Tynybraich half a century earlier. She was easy to talk and laugh with; always obliging; forever running some errand in her blue Ford Fiesta. She took meals on wheels to the "old people" of Dinas Mawddwy, though most of the recipients were years younger than her.

Olwen had a natural gift for empathy and this, along with her strong sense of independence, was the source of her quiet dignity and grace.

She died in the last year of the twentieth century. I still miss her. No day goes past without my thinking of her, wanting her company. As I take my daily walk from the end of Maesglasau valley to see Wyn and his family at Tynybraich, I think of the Olwen I knew and recall the lovely Olwen of the Mabinogion myths. Olwen: "she who leaves white traces." Wherever she walked, white clover would grow in her footsteps.

And as I walk past the fields of Maesglasau my eyes, in all their weakness, seek that modest white flower, so that I might follow the footsteps of my friend. And I would take her hand, and pull her back into this world, so that we might talk and laugh again, and share our life together in Cwm Maesglasau.

There has been much discussion about the origins of the name "Maesglasau". It was first recorded in 1425 as "Maesglasivre". It had mutated to "Maesglasfre" by 1695 and then "Maesglassey" by 1765. This suggests, say the experts, that "Maesglasfre" was the original form of the name, meaning "the meadow of the green hill". "Maesglasfre" became "Maesglase" and then "Maesglasau".

Others disagree, claiming the name is founded on a Celtic personal name, "Glasan" (comparable to the Irish name, "Glassán"), linked to the adjective "green". This name can be found in many Welsh place names, such as Pen Glason, the old name for Peniarth Hall, Bodlasan near Llanfachraeth in Anglesey, and Dôl Lasau near Bleddfa in Montgomeryshire.

The tradition in these parts is that "clas" is an element of the name, suggesting that there was a monastery at the head of the valley.

But one thing is certain, Maesglasau will be linked forever with the name of Hugh Jones, the hymn-writer. Born at the end of the cwm in 1749, he received a good education, and was a talented singer and musician. While still a young man he exchanged the quietness of Maesglasau for the noise of London. There, in the "babble and tumult of the world" he composed his first book, Cydymaith yr Hwsmon (The Companion to Husbandry), *a medley of prose and poetry, Biblical quotations and religious musings comparing the seasons of the year to the natural course of man's life . . .*

Hugh Jones returned to his birthplace to run a school. He threw himself into an intense life of writing, hymnody and translation. His publications were numerous: two volumes of poems and hymns, essays and sermons, and translations of religious, historical and medical matters. He died in penury, in the village of Henllan near Denbigh, half way through translating Isaac Watts' Y Byd a Ddaw *– (The World to Come).*

The best known hymn by Hugh Jones, Maesglasau, is "O! Tyn y Gorchudd" ("O! pull aside the veil"). Once called by the scholar, O. M. Edwards, the best hymn written in the Welsh language, it is a prayer to God for the removal on the mountain at Zion of "the veil which shrouds the people of the world". At the same time it celebrates the cleansing powers of the water on the hill at Calvary.

This is not just a reference to a verse in the Book of Isaiah. The mountain above Maesglasau, with its constant mists, must also have inspired this hymn. And the mighty waterfall in Maesglasau is surely the cleansing stream invoked by the poet.

In his hymn Hugh Jones sought a clearer vision: the removal of a veil – a curtain of darkness – from those in need of light.

This is astonishing. Hugh Jones could never have imagined that

these words would resonate with such sadness in my family home,
many generations later, in Cwm Maesglasau.

"O! PULL ASIDE THE VEIL"

O! pull aside
The veil which masks the mountain,
Let the bright white Sun of Righteousness shine down
From yonder hill, where once a gentle Lamb
Did suffer nails of steel
To show the purest love for me, in pain.

Where, where
In all the world will I find sanctuary
Else in His heavenly wounds?
The sturdy spear which tore his breast
Begat a well to cleanse me;
There is a place for me therein, and I rejoice.

Yes, yes
The bloody cross has virtuous power enough
To clean away all worldly sins:
His holy agony, his everlasting plea
Of prayer on my behalf to God
Will be my liberation, and my heavenly key.

Wash me
Of my many worldly sins
Within the crimson stream of Calvary;
A wealth of virtue in her flows today,
Ne'er shall she ebb again;
Outlasting every morning, every evening too.

5

And though the earth be barren at this time and infertile,
failing to bear fruit and flowers as it doth in the summer,
yet may we draw much sweetness from it, and hive from
it honey for the thoughtful mind, which moves the heart
to burgeon with love for the Creator.

Hugh Jones

A pall of mist conceals the cwm. I cannot see beyond it. Through
the gaps in the hazel by the stream there is nothing but white. I
cannot see beyond the mist. The light of the rush candle cannot
show me the way . . .

I take my daily walk from my home at Maesglasau Bach to
Llidiart y Dŵr, in order to strengthen my body and mind, just as
my blind brothers were taught to do at their gentlemanly school.

I know this way as I know myself, and there is no need to
grope. I have walked this path almost daily for nearly a century.
Perhaps I have become the path itself – my steps, at least – as the

flow of water becomes a stream. I could walk this path even if I too were blind.

Indeed, I am blinded by the mist today. I am the only living thing in this valley, though I can see the shades of trees, looming ghostlike, whispering silently on the periphery of my vision.

I know, too, that others stand there, in the mist, their invisible lanterns moving around me as I walk my steady path. Therefore, I am not astonished when they turn towards me, their shining lights making me close my eyes.

Sheep shine ghostly white in the gloom. Cowslip flowers glitter in the hedgerows.

I always thought that mist was cold, but it enfolds me today and keeps me warm, penetrating my old bones, warming me through. I remove my shawl and return home to drink tea and stir the fire.

I must have been daydreaming to the sound of the ticking clock. I might have dozed: it is so cosy here between the thick walls of this old house, though the fire has long since subsided. The tea in my cup is cold, a disc of light lies on its surface. The butter in a dish on the mantelpiece has melted in a golden lake. The candle has burned away.

My thoughts have been wandering all day. I must pull myself together before going for Sunday tea at Tynybraich.

I walk to the remains of the big house and raise my eyes to

the crag at Maesglasau. I watch the mist roll back from the upland, a dancer slowly raising the hem of her skirt. The mountain itself is half mist, half air, its lower slopes invisible.

I hear voices coming from the mist, telling me what it is like there. Each voice has its own vision, though none has a face.

I know that the mist will soon clear. I can feel the sun's heat pressing down on my skin. And soon I shall see a patch of grass glowing like an emerald on the upland meadow, reminding me on a grey day of mist that colours do exist.

Continuance is painful. It is the cross onto which we are tied: its beams pulling us this way and that. A longing for continuance lies at the heart of our nature, and we lie at the centre of those forces which pull us this way and that like some torturer.

Our basic urge is towards continuance. Yet, we are born to die. And we spend our lives coming to terms with that paradox. Transcendence: to put our everlasting life in the hands of a god. Displacement: to exchange subject for object and live for the land, our culture, language or fellow humans. Sublimation: to produce offspring, in the form of children, accomplishments, works of art.

The impetus of the flesh (says the Apostle) is towards death;
the impetus of the Spirit is towards life and tranquillity.

Hugh Jones

I was given a long life. It has spanned the whole of the twentieth century and has been full of experience. I have felt the rough fist of misfortune and the soft palm of joy. I have spent many hours in darkness. Yet light came anew. I learned that the price of having is losing.

Most of my contemporaries have already gone. I know that I too should accept death. Yet, I am not ready for departure. With all the strength of my frail body I crave life. As I wake each morning the beat of my heart amazes me. My faltering senses enthral me: the smell of damp earth in autumn; starry nights; the ripeness of blackberries; red berries on the hawthorn; sloes on their barbed branches.

As my days on Earth diminish my pain grows. But I do not wish God to intercede. I shall carry the cross myself. For only thus will I find rest.

And I do not wish to be buried in that graveyard at Dinas. My remains shall be scattered in the valley. For it is to Maesglasau, with its mists and waters, that I give thanks for my own life.

> The land is poor, is quiet –
> It is lonely mountain earth.
> But again the summer sews
> A glossy dress for Cwm Maesglasau;

144

Time itself just loiters here
In this land, without a care.

T. Llew Jones

I once sought my own continuance in the continuance of the cwm. In the flow of the stream and in the slant of the mountain; in blossom and leaves; in the arrival of swallows in May; in the round of the seasons and the rituals of farming; in the birth of lambs; in shearing; in reaping the hay and harvesting it; in cutting bracken on the slopes of Foel Dinas and Foel Bendin.

I sought my own continuance in the unchanging quietness of Cwm Maesglasau.

I also sought my continuance in the long-standing relationship between my family and the valley. My ancestors have farmed here for many centuries – for nearly a thousand years, according to a note in the family Bible. In 1012, says a short entry in sepia ink, a certain Gethin came to farm at Tynybraich and Maesglasau, followed by a Gruffydd who was his son, with Llywelyn following him, and so on and so on, in a family tree of fathers and grand-fathers. These men – and their women, I suppose – witnessed each revolution, renaissance and recession of this last millennium; Glyndŵr's uprising, the unification of England and Wales, the dissolution of the monasteries, the translation of God's Word into Welsh, the spreading of the gospel in printed books, the brimstone

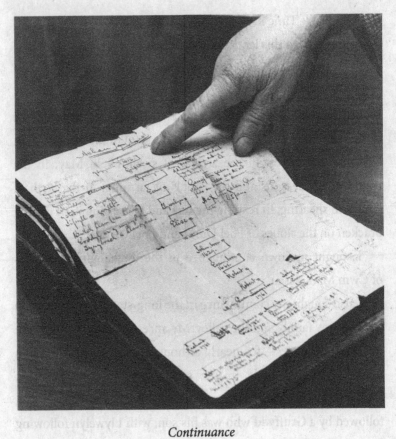

Continuance

fire of sermons; speeches and hymns, world wars, and all those revolutions in agriculture, industry, technology.

And throughout the decades of my life, I, too, have witnessed many changes. The horse-sledge was replaced by the motor car. Shire horses were replaced by the tractor. After rush lights we went on to use the candle, and then the paraffin lamp, and then electricity. Machines replaced physical beings. Instead of hands – tools. Instead of letters – the telephone. And instead of the telephone, I hear we have messages on a screen. Instead of newspapers we had radio and television. Film came to replace books. Sunday supplanted the Sabbath.

God was cast down from on high. In 1922 the first aeroplane flew over the cwm at Maesglasau. Today the Royal Air Force practises war manoeuvres in the great bowl of the cwm, its killing machines winging past us seconds before the roar, before weaving past Pen yr Allt Isaf and Pen Foel y Ffridd on their way towards Llanymawddwy.

The heavens are filled too with unseen powers, electro-magnetic waves coming from our new Gabriels.

All this has been witnessed by Cwm Maesglasau, but the cwm remains as it was. The quietness continues. My family continues: nowadays my nephew and great-nephew farm seven hundred acres in the cwm, six hundred of them mountain land. The village community still lives on; its culture alive.

And I continue to live in the remoteness of the cwm, in an old, old house. I want for nothing, other than to know that continuance lives in this land. So it was. So it is. So it shall be.

I am deceiving myself, of course. Because I cannot see the erosion of the cwm. We are all blind to the polluting forces of

147

industry, modern farming, global economics. Chernobyl. B.S.E. Foot and Mouth. The threats to indigenous flocks.

Today's mountain farmer works at a loss. Diversification is mandatory. The tradition of a thousand years risks becoming a theme park, a way of life becoming a matter of presentation. Tradition, a souvenir. The home, a guest house. The family, managers. Custom, a sentimental story. Lives repackaged as history.

The farmyards will be as empty as the meadows when the cars and buses leave.

In times such as these, continuance is a burden of conscience.

According to the entry in the family Bible, we can claim in 2012 that farming has been a way of life in Cwm Maesglasau for a thousand years. I know I shan't be there. And what of the farm?

They tell me the village is changing. Youngsters leave to seek work; the old die. Newcomers from England buy the houses: the prices are low, the views exquisite. Only a minority wish to immerse themselves in the community, and learn the Welsh language.

So, bilingualism will lead the way, until the village Eisteddfod begins to be conducted in English . . . And with it the literary society. The women's group. The gardening club. The knitting group. The drama company. The August agricultural show. The singing festival. The school concert. Children's thanksgiving. The

Christmas service at Llanymawddwy Church. On the school yard, on street corners, in the homes.

Continuance never simply continues. It is easily broken.

I have sought my own continuance in that of my family. But what comfort is that in this age of armageddon? And what right have I to expect such a thing? I did not contribute to the family – I never married; never bore children. I loved one man as I might have a husband, and lost him. In my loneliness I wrote. To create. My energy overflowed as time dried up.

> And I considered it meet to labour by day, for the night
> looms and no one can labour when darkness falls.
>
> Hugh Jones

Perhaps this was the family muse, nurtured in the cwm, calling me. The same muse as that of Hugh Jones, and my great-grand-father Evan Jones, another hymnist, and my grandfather Robert Jones the musician and his brother J. J. the poet, and his son Baldwyn the poet and dramatist.

Like Rebecca in the Book of Genesis, I felt forces in my own womb pulling me this way and that. Whether to embrace my ancestors' traditions, or reject them?

Sitting in the ruin of Maesglasau Bach, I torment myself with a pen and scraps of paper.

"CREATION"

Was it revenge to sunder the mountain in two?
Was it scorn to flood the ravine?
Violation – to bruise the glen with trees?
Deceit – your coming one day to fulfil
The silver whispers on a restless bed?
No seed was planted here by any man,
But those of hope, century upon century,
Awaiting your fruits in this fruitful cwm.

Writing an autobiography entails a "self". It entails a memory.

The remembering is easy. What else occupies the elderly? Our minds are preoccupied in part with what has passed, in part with what's to come.

I sometimes think that the act of remembering life gives more pleasure than living itself. We can select, delete, amplify, recreate, interpret memories. But life itself is unpredictable and unruly. Certain things can be recalled at will; others thrown into the bottomless pit of forgetting. We can choose when to laugh and to cry; when to challenge and to submit. Such is the privilege of remembering.

And the self? Which "self" should I remember? I never gave it much thought. It never bothered me much, except when it got hurt. Its form is outlined by other selves: those of my family and friends, the cwm, my writing.

I was a seamstress throughout my life. Today I see before me a patchwork quilt of memories. It keeps me warm in my last winter. My "self" lies perhaps in the act of sewing the seams, and in the seams themselves. The material is there: remnants of clothing worn by family and friends; broadcloth from the world; the shimmering satin of Cwm Maesglasau; the velvet of tranquillity.

It is composed of contradictory elements.

But no, I deceive myself again. In this case I am not a seamstress. For the quilt is made of paper. Written words are the material's print. The thread: my family's story. The seams: the clauses of generations. The stitches themselves: life's mutations; the mutation which impelled me to seek tranquillity at the far end of Cwm Maesglasau, which forced Bob to become an unwilling farmer, and which exiled Gruffydd, William and Lewis from the cwm, compelling one to become an Anglican vicar in England, another a gifted linguist with a dozen languages in his possession, and the last a prize-winning painter.

This work is unfinished. And thus it will remain until the end of the family, until the end of the cwm.

My own work on it has almost ended. All I need to do is sew the lining, to conceal the seams and to make it soft on the skin when I rest shrouded beneath it.

Only one material will do for that lining. It is a rather special material which cannot be seen, heard, touched, tasted nor smelled.

I believe that I am on the verge of finding it. Was it not yesterday that it flowed past, meandering away from me towards the big field?

Unexpectedly, it was the rain that came after the mist. It poured down, drowning the land. The stream increased in volume and breadth.

It rained and rained, beating down on the old monks of Cwm Maesglasau, in retribution for their sins:

> Rain comes from the dampness and wetness of the earth
> and sea; and is raised to the sky by the heat of the sun,
> where it mingles and forms clouds; and after that, by the
> will of the lord above, it is released and falls down on the
> earth again in cascading showers.
>
> Hugh Jones

I walk through that downpour towards Llidiart y Dŵr, and rejoice as I approach my kin at Tynybraich. And the rain flows down my cheeks, as though the stream itself were flowing over me, baptising me into another life.

Rebecca Jones died of diphtheria in 1916.
She was eleven years old. This book is a
tribute to the life she might have lived.

AFTERWORD

What makes a novel a classic? Usually it's a lengthy process, involving a sustained period of critical and popular acclaim, but *O! Tyn y Gorchudd* was hailed as a classic on its first appearance and promptly awarded the National Eisteddfod Prose Medal in 2002, and the Welsh-language Book of the Year Award in 2003. Abroad it made its author the first Welsh-language writer to be promoted by Scritture Giovani, an E.U.-sponsored initiative; at home it has been adapted for radio and discussed by bloggers as the "first masterpiece of the twenty-first century", while passages from it have been chosen as competitive "recitation pieces" – the mark of a popularly acknowledged classic if ever there was one. What is it about this novel, then, which gained for it such rapid and widespread recognition as a "classic"?

The answer lies perhaps in the relation between the lyrically evoked rural Welsh lifestyle portrayed in the body of the text and the startling twist to the whole narrative given in the final few sentences. Throughout her story the narrator presents herself as embedded within her family – farmers in the Maesglasau valley for a thousand years – and within the history of that valley and its Welsh-speaking community: she saw her own continuation in the valley's continuation. Consequently, her sudden dissolution at the close seems to eradicate more than herself alone. Momentarily it is as if the continuation of Welsh-language culture in the twentieth century has abruptly been exposed as a mirage, a dream that never was; it all ended back in 1916, during those corrosive First World War years. The reader flounders in a strange vacuum, before recognising that only one voice has in fact been lost in this instance, and the relief makes the actual reality of twentieth-century Welsh rural culture as it has been represented throughout the rest of the text by contrast all the more precious, as well as all the more vulnerable. In this context, the very title of the novel – "*O! Tyn y Gorchudd*" ("O! pull aside the veil") – seems to refer not only to the physical blindness of the narrator's brothers but also to the psychological blindness of those who remain unaware of the value of their linguistic culture and its peril. It is because it manages thus to awaken once again, in a manner which is un-expected and new, the sense of combined celebration and dread in relation to Welsh-language culture that this novel seems so straightforwardly a successor to those earlier twentieth-century classics which struck similar chords, Kate Roberts' *Traed Mewn Cyffion* (*Feet in Chains*, 1936), for example, Islwyn Ffowc Elis' *Wythnos yng Nghymru Fydd* (*A Week in the Wales of the Future*, 1957), or Angharad Tomos' *Yma o Hyd* (*Still Here*, 1985).

The way in which its subject is its language has, however, led some of its readers to view this novel as untranslatable. "This is the strongest argument I've seen for a while for securing the survival of the Welsh language – after all, *O! Tyn y Gorchudd* wouldn't work in another language" comments one blogger on the maes-e.com website. Yet its translator Lloyd Jones, himself a master of the novelist's craft, succeeds in that difficult task of conveying the poetry of the original while adhering at the same time very closely to its literal meaning. Many of the finest qualities of the text – the poignancy of the brothers' blindness, the evocation of the landscape and its seasons, the accuracy and freshness of the metaphors – the hawk "a steel bullet sheathed in feathers" ("*bwled dur o blu*"), for example – are very effectively transposed.

One aspect of the book in translation may, however, not "work" for its English readers, and yet the very difficulty reveals all the more tellingly the nature of the culture represented in the original. The text's narrative voice is very erudite: Rebecca has a wealth of Welsh- and English-language culture at her command and makes passing reference to an array of literary and historical sources, from W. B. Yeats to Taliesin and R. T. Jenkins. Given that she is by profession a seamstress, with no education beyond that of the village school, it's likely that her tone will strike readers who tend to think stereotypically of the connections between culture, class and material wealth as unexpected. In fact the text discloses in some detail how Rebecca acquired her learning: her Sunday School teacher, who was also her uncle, made his class learn Welsh and English poems, "not all of them Christian", by rote every week; her grandfather was too voracious a reader to be a successful farmer, but left a rich store of books to be inherited by Rebecca and her brothers, along with an appetite for reading to be satisfied later by the local public library; throughout her life she took great pleasure in talking to her brothers about books, on the telephone if not face to face. All the same her voice is likely to sound too highbrow to be readily credible to an English-language reader as that of a seamstress in straitened circumstances, but the same difficulty is not evident in Welsh.

Another feature which underlines the authenticity of the text is the fact that Rebecca's family is the novelist's: the grandniece Angharad, fleetingly referred to in chapter five, is the same Angharad as the one on the title page. Apart from the single exception exposed at the close, the details of the family history are fact not fiction. And yet this book is a novel, and a fine one too: to write one's family history in such a way that it is instantly hailed as a literary classic is a remarkable achievement. In the pages which follow, a rich reading experience awaits those who have not previously made the acquaintance of Rebecca Jones of Maesglasau.

JANE AARON

TRANSLATOR'S NOTES

As soon as I read Angharad's book, I knew it was a pocket masterpiece which deserved a wider audience. And I really enjoyed the experience of translating it: I only hope that I've done it justice. Of course, no translation can truly capture the original, especially a book which is so quintessentially Welsh as *O! Tyn y Gorchudd*. I wanted to mirror its sensitivity, its shyness, its quiet reflectiveness and its ancient dignity. A book further away from *Trainspotting* you couldn't wish to find.

Maesglasau is a living, breathing place, and this book portrays a way of life which is disappearing quickly, whilst also recognising the valley as an arena for eternity itself. Quietly, the people go about their daily lives – but they are capable of heroism and deep compassion; somehow they're aware that time is a great silver web stretching away into the far distance, and they can only marvel at its artistry before they're caught in it themselves, after a lifetime of hard work and spiritual endeavour.

So this is the story of a beautiful valley and an amazing family, both ordinary and extraordinary, with three blind brothers and a gift for languages; the story of a mountain stream as it journeys towards the sea, and the story of an upland tribe as it journeys towards a new world.

Seemingly simple, it has a deceptive depth: many people feel that they've read a substantial saga rather than a slim volume.

At the end of his Booker prize-winner *The Sea*, John Banville uses a simple analogy to capture a deep emotional insight: he describes the way a wave can pick you up when you're standing in the sea and suddenly deposit you elsewhere. That's the feeling I had when I'd finished reading this book: it took my breath away.

I hope you enjoy this book as much as its original readers have, since it is one of the most respected and popular publications of recent times. Indeed, many readers have been impelled to visit the valley after reading about it. Like me they have responded to the book's finely wrought craftsmanship and its simple intimacy; it's as though the story had been written by a member of your own family.

I commend it to you.

LLOYD JONES
Llanfairfechan, February 2010

A GUIDE TO THE PRONUNCIATION OF WELSH

Welsh spelling is regular and phonetic, so that once you know the rules, you can pronounce it without too much difficulty. Words are usually stressed on the penultimate syllable.

Vowels: a, e, i, o, u, w, y

a, as in *man*

e, as in *met*

i, as the *ee* in *queen*

o, as in *hot*

u, as the *i* in *bit*

w, as the *oo* in *zoo*

y can be pronounced either as *uh* or as *i* in *bit*

And combinations of vowels:

ae, *ai* and *au* all pronounced approximately as in *eye*

aw, as in *now*

eu and *ei*, as in *say*

ew is pronounced *eh-oo*

iw and *yw* are pronounced *ee-oo*

oe is pronounced *oh-eh*

ow, as in *throw*

wy is pronounced *oo-ee* (or sometimes as in *win*)

Vowels can be lengthened by adding a circumflex accent (^)

Consonants (b, d, h, l, m, n, p, s, t are pronounced as in English)

c, always hard as in *cat*

ch, aspirated as in the Scottish *loch*

dd, as the *th* in *the*

f, as the *v* in *vet*

ff, as the *f* in *from*

g, always hard as in *go*

ng, as the *ng* in *finger*

ll is peculiarly Welsh and resembles an aspirated *l* (blow around side of tongue)

ph, as in *phonetic*

r is rolled, as in Spanish or Italian

rh is pronounced with an *h* sound produced before the *r*

th as *th* in *thanks*